Mason Valley Ranch

by

Lynn Medley

DORRANCE PUBLISHING CO., INC.
PITTSBURGH, PENNSYLVANIA 15222

This is a work of fiction. Names, characters, places, and incidents are either the product of the author's imagination or are used fictitiously, and any resemblance to actual persons, living or dead; events; or locales is entirely coincidental.

All Rights Reserved
Copyright © 2007 by Lynn Medley
No part of this book may be reproduced or transmitted
in any form or by any means, electronic or mechanical,
including photocopying, recording, or by any information
storage and retrieval system without permission in
writing from the publisher.

ISBN: 978-0-8059-7578-9

Library of Congress Control Number: 2006939702

Printed in the United States of America

First Printing

For more information or to order additional books, please contact:
Dorrance Publishing Co., Inc.
701 Smithfield Street
Third Floor
Pittsburgh, Pennsylvania 15222
U.S.A.
1-800-788-7654
www.dorrancebookstore.com

*To Jean, for her patience,
understanding, and all the time alone.*

Chapter One

The car slowly drove through the gates of the cemetery and turned left at the last intersection. The old wooden bridge over the dry wash groaned loudly with the weight of the vehicle and creaked as the last two tires found pavement again. There was another turn left onto a short dirt road before the car stopped. The driver opened her door and walked around the front of the car to open the door for her passenger. The old woman in the car grabbed the arm of the driver and stood up to steady herself before the long walk up the path to the grave. Neither of them spoke during the walk. The old woman gave a vase of flowers to the driver then sat down on a large rock. She kissed the vase before placing it next to the headstone.

"Are you sure you won't need any help, Mama?" the driver asked. "I hate to leave you out here alone like this."

"I'll be fine, honey, don't you worry." The old woman waved her hand at her daughter as if to say get along. "Birdie and I talk better when we're alone."

"I'll get the other things you brought for her." The driver walked back to the car and opened the trunk. She took out a shovel, a bucket of water, and a cottonwood sapling. "You know the doctor wants you to rest." She set the items down next to the old woman. "I don't think you should be doing this by yourself."

"I'll have plenty of time to rest when my time comes."

"Don't say that." The driver brushed a few strands of hair away from the old woman's eyes. "I'll be back in a while then."

The old woman watched the car disappear on the tree-lined streets. In the Indian cemetery there were no trees for shade and no neatly manicured grass like in the white man's area. Another injustice to Birdie and her people, the old woman mumbled to herself.

"Guess it's hot enough for you today, huh?" She took off her cowboy hat and wiped her brow with her arm. "No weeds allowed around here."

She leaned over the grave and plucked out the weeds. "I'll not have anything but pretty flowers near you, sweetheart. Rachel brought me. She said to say hello and she hopes you enjoy the flowers. We bought them together. She misses you so much. It's kinda hard on me too cause I see so much of you in her every day, and its hard not to call her by your name. I brought you a cottonwood for some shade. This sapling is from the one behind the back porch. You know the one you planted after the trial. I'm not a spry as I used to be so I'd better be getting this in the ground before the sun makes the dirt as hard as a rock."

When the younger woman returned to the grave she saw that her mother was leaning against the headstone asleep. She picked up the bucket and poured the last of the water onto the sapling. She read the inscription etched in the marble stone:

Singing Bird Perez 1869 - 1939

"You two always did things differently and I think the spirits are getting a little nervous about Mama getting close to joining you. I doubt they will be able to handle you two any more than these mortals did."

"Did you say something to me?" The old woman held her hat up to the sun to block the sun from her eyes.

"No Mama, I was taking to Birdie," she said as she

stamped the dirt around the sapling with her foot.

"She just loves this, you know."

"She deserves better than this." The old woman pointed to the bare cemetery.

"Indians still don't count for too much according to most people, Mama. You are one of but a very few that thinks differently. Maybe someday it will come about. Maybe in my children's lifetime. It's getting too hot for you to be out in the sun."

The old woman kissed her fingertips and pressed them against the headstone. "Well Birdie, it's time for me to go again. Take care of your tree, and I'll be back soon."

The old woman sat down in the car seat. "It's a damned shame for all of them." She watched as Birdie's headstone disappear behind her. "Let's get home before I get really mad and go to city hall about it."

"Mama, have you thought any more about our conversation we had the other day when I asked you about your life in the valley? I got a little from Birdie in the last years before she passed away, but she said you would be better to tell it. There is still so much I still don't know about her. She seemed to be really embarrassed to talk about it. She told me about living here on the ranch until she was seventeen then she wouldn't tell me any more. She said that some things were better left in the past. She's been gone for over a year now and people still talk about her. Here I am, a grown woman with children of my own and I can't tell them where they come from because I still don't know."

The old woman looked out the side window of the car at the sun as it hovered above the mountain ridge and remembered how much Birdie loved the desert sunsets.

"My life on the ranch was hard, but hers was impossible. I don't know if I could've gone through what she did and survived."

The car turned into the driveway to the ranch. The young woman knew from experience that her mother would say nothing until she was ready. She knew that the woman she called mother had adopted her and that Birdie was her birth mother. She had heard stories from other tribal members when she visited the reservation, but nothing was ever said at the ranch, even when she asked. She shared the same name, Rachel, as her adopted mother.

The old woman reached over and touched her daughter's arm. "Help an old lady into the house."

When she sat down in a large over stuffed chair she held on to her daughter's hand. "If you make me a good strong cup of Jack Daniel's with a drop coffee in it maybe you can get me to tell you about her."

She watched her daughter walk into the kitchen then leaned back in the chair and smiled while her mind drifted back to the time her father came to Mason Valley.

Chapter Two

Sean O'Callahan came west to get away from the Civil War. Adele, my mother, came with him but not with the blessings of her family. She was from a prominent family in Pennsylvania, and they weren't too keen on her marrying someone they thought below her station. Before the war in Iowa, she had entered her prized stallion in a race. She met Sean when they both had been assigned the same horse stall. He gave her the stall, but she was taken by his good looks and manners. Their horses were entered in the same race. She won, and he graciously accepted defeat so she asked him to an afternoon meal for being so good about it.

It wasn't long before she was head over heels in love with Sean and introduced him to her father. He tried to keep them apart, but his efforts only made her more determined than ever to be with Sean. He chased her back to Sean's farm to take her back home, but it was too late as they were already married. Her father tried to pay Sean to get an annulment, but he refused. Her father never forgave her for eloping, but when the grandchildren came along he softened up a bit.

Life was fine until the war broke out. Her father was a union supporter, but Sean didn't take sides. He didn't support slavery, but he couldn't see brothers killing brothers over a different point of view. Sean and Adele's father couldn't talk about anything without a heated discussion starting up about the war. Sean finally put the farm up for sale in '61 and sold it just as the war was escalating. They bought a Conestoga wagon, packed their things, and headed west. At Salt Lake City they heard about the silver mines in Virginia City and land to be had for farming.

They knew people would be there for mining and would need food to live. They left the wagon train and set out for Virginia City. They heard about homesteading land in the Mason Valley and applied for a grant. They worked the land and as other farmers and ranchers caught silver fever Sean bought their land as they left. One thing he learned was the climate was a lot different than Iowa's. He tried to grow several different kinds of crops, but alfalfa grew the best. He became the largest alfalfa supplier to ranchers all around the northern Nevada area. He also became a cattle rancher as beef was in high demand in Virginia City. He kept buying land and building the ranch, and before too long he owned half of the valley.

The Mexican and Indian hired hands who worked on the ranches that were sold to Sean stayed to work for him. He built bunkhouses for the single men and cabins for men with families. In the summer of the second year a son, Jacob, was born. One afternoon in the fall Adele was cooking at the wood stove when she noticed an Indian man standing outside the door of the kitchen. She asked him what he wanted, but he didn't speak to her. He turned and pointed to a small group of women and children behind him then rubbed his stomach. One woman who was heavy with child stood in the yard with three other women and six children behind her. From their clothes Adele guessed that they had been walking for quite a spell. She opened the door to let them in, but they backed up and huddled close to each other. Adele asked the man if he could understand anything she was saying but he only pointed at his stomach and at the others.

Finally one of the women asked if they could have some food in a language that sounded like French. Adele had learned French in boarding school, and although she was a bit rusty at it she told the woman that they all could go into the house and get something to eat. The woman said they would just like some food and then would be on their way. Suddenly the young pregnant woman screamed and fell to the ground. The other women tried to help her up. Adele called for some of the hired hands to get the woman into the kitchen. As they lay the woman on the floor she gave birth to a baby girl. Adele didn't give the tiny child much of a chance, but the child kept fighting for breath. The rest of the small band had entered the kitchen to watch so Adele gave all of them some food. Sean came in from the barn and was startled to see all of them in the kitchen. Adele shrugged her shoulders at him as she set a place for him at the table. She also told the woman who spoke French that the group could stay in the barn for the night and could stay at the ranch until the woman with the baby was ready to travel. The woman talked to the small group, and they left the kitchen leaving behind the woman with the baby.

"We can't take care of them, Adele," Sean said.

"Just look at them. They are shabby and obviously hungry. We...I can't just let them go to who knows what."

"They got traditions they got to follow. They aren't like the Indians we have here on the ranch."

"Their traditions are being taken away more and more, Sean. I wonder how they will be able to continue living like that."

The baby cried and the mother put it to her breast. Even though she and Adele couldn't speak the same language Adele knew the Indian woman was embarrassed to be in their kitchen.

"Just look at her, Sean. She's just a baby herself. How can I let her go into the unknown with that baby?"

"It ain't our place to take care of them, Adele. They got to figure it out by themselves. We got Indians that work on the ranch now that didn't want to stay that way. They figured out that things change and sometimes the change is better than the old ways."

"Well I ain't going to let that baby ail while it's in our house. I will make a bed here in the kitchen by the stove so they both can be warm tonight."

The next morning the small group stood at the back door for food and the leader spoke to the baby's mother. Adele knew the baby wasn't healthy enough to travel and understood by the tone of the conversation that the group was not going to stay and wait for the baby to get better. The woman who spoke French told Adele they had to leave or they would be too far behind the rest of the travelers. Adele asked about the father and would he be able to come and get the mother and girl. The father had been killed in a skirmish with cavalry troops a few months earlier and they had taken her in. The old man at the door was her uncle, and he said that if she couldn't walk then she would be left behind. A small band like them would be prey for bounty hunters. The young woman cried when the others walked out of the kitchen and down the road. She called to the band several times then resigned herself that they weren't coming back or that she couldn't go with them. Adele sat down and wrapped her arms around her.

The woman stayed in the kitchen for a few days then Adele took her across the yard to an old cabin. They might not have understood each other's language, but they were both mothers and knew that a baby should have a good warm place to stay if it was to get better. As Little Bird regained her strength she started helping Adele with her chores to pay for Sean and Adele's kindness. Joachim, one of the ranch hands, acted as a translator for her and Adele. He told Adele the woman's name was Little Bird and she was a Paiute from the big spring's area north of Rag Town. She had married her husband two years ago and was living with his family at the lake of the cui-ui. He took an interest in the woman and started helping her get the cabin cleaned out. Before long they were living together, and he adored the little baby girl because she always laughed when he picked her up and babbled whenever she heard a bird chirping. Her mother called her Singing Bird, but he called her Birdie.

Over the next few years Little Bird gave birth to Little Joachim and Alejandro. Adele gave birth to me on the same day Little Bird gave birth to Alejandro. Adele and Little Bird became close friends, and the children grew up as one big family. Life on a ranch was hard, especially the biggest ranch in the valley, but when all the chores were done then it was time to have fun.

The towns of Yerington and Wabuska were taking off as the railroads came through. The mines in Virginia City were still going strong, and the city needed beef and other supplies from the surrounding valleys. Fort Lyon also needed beef, and we supplied most of what was needed to them, too. The valley was growing so much that Pa and Mr. Jamison, who owned the ranch to the east, decided to build a schoolhouse. While it was being built a teacher was hired from Maryland, and until she arrived the children took lessons from Ma in the parlor using some of her old school books. It was a big deal when the school opened that year. We all were so happy to have a real schoolhouse and see all the other children from the valley. I sat next to Birdie. She was like a sister to me and we did everything together. Birdie learned how to live in my world, and I learned how to live in hers.

Right about my seventeenth year things started to change for all of us. We had heard about some skirmishes between the miners and some Indians up north. Some of the people here in the valley feared an Indian uprising and told Pa his Indian workers weren't welcome in town anymore. Because the government was rounding up all the Indians not on a reservation, Pa told his hired hands to stay on the ranch property. One afternoon the cavalry showed up at the ranch. They rode up to the house and stopped when the lieutenant raised his hand. He dismounted and walked up the stairs and knocked on the door. Ma couldn't have known that when she opened the door that day that things would never be the same again.

"Hello ma'am, I am Lieutenant Montgomery and I am here as a representative of the U.S. government. I need to talk to your husband. Is he here?"

Adele stepped outside the door. "My husband is in town at the moment and won't be back until this evening. Can I help you?"

"I think I should talk to your husband regarding this matter, ma'am."

"You can talk to me, Lieutenant. We both know why you're here. The Indians who live here on the ranch have been here for years and you have no need to take them."

"Ma'am, I have orders to round up all the Indians in this valley and get them to Fort Lyon."

"You can't possibly wait until my husband gets back?"

The lieutenant mounted his horse. He was losing patience with Adele. "Mrs. O'Callahan, I intend to be back at the fort tonight. If I get these Indians and leave pretty soon my men can be in their own quarters."

"What about my friends? Where will they sleep tonight?"

"Don't you worry about them. We have made arrangements, and they will be taken care of."

Adele stepped off of the porch. "I have heard about your arrangements and I don't like them."

"Mrs. O'Callahan," the lieutenant's voice raised up in volume as he spoke, "I am not here to discuss policy with a man's wife. I am here to get Indians, and I will have my men tear this place apart to look for them if need be."

"Adele." Little Bird and Joachim were standing at the corner of the house. "I will go with them."

"No, Little Bird," Adele said. "I won't let them take my friend."

Little Bird walked over to Adele and put a hand on her shoulder. "I don't want any harm to come to you or the ranch."

Joachim stood next to Little Bird. "If you take her than you must take me, too."

"Who the hell are you?" The lieutenant asked.

"I am Joachim Perez. She is my woman."

The lieutenant took off his hat and wiped his brow with his handkerchief.

"Suit yourself, old man." Glancing around the rest of the yard he asked, "Are there any children?"

"No..." Adele spoke very fast and looked at Little Bird hoping she wouldn't say anything. "No children here but my own."

The lieutenant flopped his hat back on his head. "We were told that there were Indian children."

"The only children here are my own." Adele walked up the steps to the porch and opened the screen door. "If you don't believe me then look any place you want on the ranch."

The lieutenant didn't believe her, but he could always come another day. "No ma'am, I think this will do. I am warning you, however, that if there are any Indian children on the ranch and you are hiding them, you will be arrested. We need to keep track of the Indians for the good of the territory."

"I'll get them some provisions before you go."

"Ma'am, they're not to have anything with them when they get to the fort. That way they we don't have any problems."

"Surely they can have some warm blankets and clothing," Adele said even though she knew the answer.

"The government will provide everything they will need, Mrs. O'Callahan." The lieutenant was getting very tired of talking to her.

Adele gave Joachim a hug and kissed his forehead. "Sean will come get you as soon as he knows."

"Tell my children that I love them," Little Bird whispered.

She cried when she hugged Little Bird. "I will take care of your children. I promise."

The lieutenant ordered the men to form two lines with Little Bird and Joachim between them when he gave the orders to leave. Adele watched them until she could no longer see them.

She was sitting in the rocker on the porch when Sean put the wagon in the barn and walked across the yard to the house.

"They came and took Little Bird and Joachim."

"Who did?" Sean asked.

"The Lieutenant from Fort Lyon and some men. I tried to get them to wait until you got back, but I couldn't."

He put his hands on her shoulders. "I'll go to town tomorrow and send a wire to the governor. If I have to I'll go see the commander of the fort myself to get them back."

"At least they didn't get the children. They should be in from the east meadows this evening." She put her head on his shoulder and cried. "I don't know how to tell them."

Chapter Three

The sagebrush slapped and scratched at the sides of Rachel's legs. Her chaps were scarred and stained after years of riding the hills looking for cattle. Even sitting high on a horse wasn't enough to escape it. It grew dense and thick and the cows seemed to relish laying in it. She nudged Jester, her horse, a little further up the hill and scared out two pregnant cows. She stopped to watch Birdie and Jacob get three more out of a small ravine. They pushed them towards the larger herd in a pen at the end of the meadow. Alejandro opened a wire gate to let them in with the rest of the herd.

"Anybody seen Joachim lately?" Jacob asked.

"He was out there wrangling with four more or so," Birdie pointed to the other end of the meadow. "They weren't being too cooperative either."

"Leave him to get a knot-headed bunch," Jacob said. "Alejandro and I will go look over by the river. You two keep a lookout for him here."

He motioned for Alejandro to follow him then raced off.

Rachel watched him ride off and thought how much he looked like their father. He was still a bit gangly with his youth but growing into a good sized body. With thick red hair like their father's and a soft spoken voice, he was the heartthrob of all the girls in the valley. Whoever caught and married Jacob O'Callahan would be the queen of the valley as he was the heir to the ranch. Thank goodness Rachel had auburn hair and her mother's German stature and no freckles. Irish and German heritage made them both a little taller than most, and as her mother always said, big boned. She herself had grown a lot the last year or so. Her mother had to keep letting her blouses and trousers out to keep up with her growth. Finally she had to start wearing hand me downs from her father and Jacob, and that suited her just fine. The other kids at school teased her a lot, but she didn't care.

"Rachel, do you want to go to the hot springs after we get home? We haven't been there for a spell," Birdie said as she brushed dust off of her hat. "This damned dirt gets into every part of my body and I want to be clean. I'm tired of grinding my skin off every time I brush this stuff off."

"Yeah…why not," Rachel said. "But we have to make sure the boys aren't going, though."

"What's wrong with them coming along?"

"You know damned well why not." Rachel blushed.

"What's the matter, Rachel?" Birdie laughed. "There's no reason to get upset about growing out of your blouses. Every girl does that when she becomes a woman. I did."

"I don't like them teasing me." Rachel scowled. "Besides, Ma says that we shouldn't go with them anymore because of them growing up, too."

"My mother says that women should be careful of men." Birdie dismounted and brushed more dirt off. "She says that they cause a lot of problems for women and do some very stupid things. I asked her what she meant, and she said that I will soon find out. I told her that I do not like boys. She said that I am still young and I will change my mind when I grow up a little bit more. Well I have grown up and I still do not like them."

Rachel watched Birdie slap the dust off of her clothes. She liked watching Birdie. She had always liked to watch Birdie. She wondered if she would change when she got a little older.

"Oh look, there they are." Birdie mounted her horse. "Now

we can get home."

The strays were stopped short of the pen so Rachel could open the gate. Birdie rode to the back of the pen to make sure all of the cows were out. Rachel stayed at the tail end of the herd to make sure no strays got away. She thought about when she and Birdie were younger. No matter if they were doing chores or just playing around she would always make sure she was with Birdie. As the years went by she felt the need to watch over Birdie and protect her. Not that Birdie needed to be protected. She could take care of herself and had proven it many times over the years. One of the cows bolted out of the herd down a gully, and she spurred Jester after him. "Get back in there you mangy heifer." She grabbed the rope that was hanging from the saddle horn and waved it in the air to scare the cow back up the side of the gully.

She thought about the hot springs and how things had changed. They had always gone there to play and relax when they were younger, but the last year or so she had been having uncertain feelings about being there with the others. Sure, she was growing up, but so were they and they didn't seem to care how each of them changed. Maybe it was because of the teasing she got from the other kids at the schoolhouse. Maybe it was the feeling she got when Birdie undressed and jumped into the pond. She made sure that she always got undressed after Birdie then would make sure she was the first one dressed so she could watch her comb her long black hair while sitting in the sun. She wasn't sure what it all meant, but her heart would start pounding and her stomach would start churning. No, she wasn't real sure what it all meant, but she knew that she really liked being around Birdie.

Alejandro raced ahead to open the gate to the stock pens. Rachel closed it after the last cow had rumbled through. She walked Jester into the barn to put him in his stall. Adele and Sean were talking to Birdie, Joachim, and Alejandro.

"Rachel, you might want to come here and hear this."

"What Pa?" She saw that Birdie and her brothers were

crying.

"I have some real bad news for Joachim, Birdie, and Alejandro."

"What?"

"The cavalry came and took Joachim and Little Bird this morning. They will take them to the reservation up north."

"Why didn't somebody come and get us?" Birdie asked. "We could've been here with them."

"They would've taken you, too." Adele put her arms around Birdie. "Your mother was glad they didn't get you. I told her I would take care of you, and I will. She said to tell you that she loves you."

"Maybe we can go and get them," Joachim said.

"No son, it won't be possible," Sean said. "All that will accomplish is that they will have you, too."

"What are we gonna do, Pa?" Jacob asked. "We got to get them back."

"Tomorrow I am going to Carson City to see the governor and try to bring them back here. Right now all we can do is hope."

Jacob shook his head. "How can they come on our ranch and take them like that?"

"Jacob, there are a lot of people that are afraid of Indians right now. They want them to be accounted for and this is how the government does it."

"What about them?" Rachel asked. "Everyone in this valley knows they live here. How do we protect them?"

"We will cross that bridge when we come to it. If they think that the cavalry took you then it will be easier to keep you here. From now on the three of you will stay on the ranch. Jacob and Rachel will give you the lessons from school." Adele put a hand on Alejandro and Birdie's shoulders. "We will move the three of you to the main house." Adele walked to the door of the barn. "Now go and get your things. I know this is hard, but you must be brave for your mother."

Birdie told Alejandro and Joachim to start getting their things from the cabin. She walked across the yard to the orchard. From the time they were babies her mother would sit in the orchard in the evening and sing songs and tell stories about how the Great Spirit would bring the flowers in the spring and how they attracted the bees and birds. Eventually the flowers would become fruit to be eaten and that was how the Great Spirit took care of his people. She walked down several rows, remembering all the stories her mother told again and again but they always listened as if it was for the first time. She sat down on the old log her mother sat on when she told the stories.

After helping the boys get their things from the cabin, Rachel walked to the orchard.

"Is there anything I can do to help Birdie?" Rachel asked.

"I'll never hear her stories again, Rachel."

"Don't say that, Birdie."

"All I can see is black."

"We'll bring them back, Birdie. We'll get them back."

"My mind is full of black."

"We have to get your stuff. The boys have finished."

Rachel followed Birdie to the cabin but didn't go inside. After a long wait she walked into the cabin and saw Birdie sitting next to a large cedar chest with the lid raised. She was holding a winnowing basket in her arms and rocking back and forth.

"I remember when she put this in here. Mother called this box a hope chest. She learned about it from your mother and was getting these things ready for me when I married." She rubbed the winnowing basket with her fingers. "Here is the little girl dress she made for me with the material your mother ordered for her. She helped me make this buckskin dress from the deer that Joachim got last year. She did the beadwork herself. I told her it was too big but she told me it would fit in due time and that when I wore it I would give my heart to the one I love forever."

She wrapped her arms around the dress.

Rachel wanted to comfort her but didn't know what to do. Birdie walked around the cabin, trying to decide what she would take with her. Still clutching the dress she stopped in front of Rachel and laid her head on her shoulder and cried.

"I wish I could change it back, Birdie. Your family belongs here with us and not on some reservation. Maybe Pa can talk to the governor and make him see it's not fair."

"It was just a matter of time and we all knew it. I should've been here with them."

"No. You would be gone, too, and I couldn't stand that...I mean that we couldn't stand that. You belong here with me...us."

"I belong with my family."

"I thought we were your family."

"You know what I mean, Rachel." Birdie pushed the door open and walked to the main house. Rachel looked around the cabin and slowly closed the door.

Chapter Four

Winter had been unusually harsh and with Little Bird and Joachim gone it seemed even worse. The spring thaw was starting in the valley, and with so much do to it would help them not to think or dwell on what had happened. After the cows had finished dropping their calves and the branding was done, the plan, as usual, was to get them back to the high country for the summer. This year Jacob, Joachim, and Alejandro would drive the main herd with Rachel and Birdie to follow with the late arrivals.

Rachel closed the gate after the last of the cows had past her and wondered how many more times it would happen. People all over the territory couldn't talk about anything but the Indians and wanted them accounted for. She and Jacob had been asked if Birdie and her brothers were gone. They just said that the cavalry had been out to the ranch. They heard in town that the cavalry had been sent up north because of some fighting between settlers and Indians. Just stay up north, she thought as she pushed the gate closed and waited for the hasp to clunk into position.

"Rachel, want to go the hot springs?" Birdie asked as she walked up to the gate. "The boys are gone now."

"I have to treat some of the cows yet."

"I know, but I thought that when you were through you could meet me. We haven't been up there this year yet, and

I sure would like to get into that warm water."

Rachel was glad to see Birdie smile. It had been a very long winter and with all the dark cold days it sometimes seemed as if Birdie didn't want to go on living. She had resigned herself that nothing could be changed especially when Sean came back from Carson City and told them he couldn't bring Little Bird and Joachim back. She still had her bad days, and Rachel would sit alongside her while she talked about things.

"Go on ahead then. Why don't you ask Ma if she has anything we can take to eat?"

"Good, I'll get some towels and a blanket." Birdie ran towards the house.

"Are you sure it's a good thing to go to the springs?" Adele wiped her hands on a towel. I worry about the two of you alone out there."

"Ma, we can take care of ourselves. Besides its Birdie's idea and she is finally getting to be her old self again. I'll take Luke and the rifle with me."

"I can't keep her and her brothers locked up in the house, I guess, so go and have a good time."

Rachel gave Adele a hug. "I promise we'll be back at dusk."

She saddled Jester and rode to the springs through the meadows. She liked this time of year in the meadows because the birds were nesting and the deer came out of the brush to drink from the creeks. A fawn started to jump and bounce around next to its mother then splashed into the water. She wondered if the red-tailed hawks that were soaring above her were the same ones that nested in the old cottonwood tree for the last three years.

This part of the ranch would someday be hers. Jacob would get the larger piece of the ranch when the time came, but this section had already been promised to her. It was a benefit that the hot springs were on this piece of property. It was curious that the hot springs would be not too far from cold water pond and neither one ran into the other. Sean said that it had something to do with the Sierra's being so close to the earthquakes in the San Joaquin Valley on the west side of the mountain range. She didn't really understand it all that much, but it felt good to swim in them, and that's all she cared about. She followed the small trail that wound around the ponds and stopped at a clearing between them. She took the saddle off of Jester and put it on an old, bleached out log. Walking to the pond, she started to call out to Birdie but instead decided to sit on a stump to watch her swim. The steam curled up above the water with each stroke of her arms. She disappeared below the surface for a moment then walked to a large rock that was partially submerged. She lay down on the rock to let the sun dry her body.

A red-tailed hawk called out from the sky. Rachel looked up at it and watched it drift on the wind currents. She wondered if this place had always been this beautiful and why she hadn't noticed it before. This was their hideaway from the world. She and Birdie had shared their innermost secrets and girlhood thoughts here.

"Rachel...are you all right?" Birdie was standing next to Rachel with a blanket wrapped around her shoulders.

"Yeah, I...uh was just thinking."

"I guess so. I called you several times, but you didn't hear me. What has you so deep in thought?"

"I was just wondering what it would be like to fly like that hawk up there. I wonder what he sees."

"Rachel, you are always thinking, aren't you? Not a minute goes by that you aren't thinking of something or another. Well stop thinking and get into the water. It feels really good today." She dropped the blanket as she walked back to the pond.

"I don't think I'll get in today. I have to go back to the ranch...there's something I forgot to do."

Birdie walked back. "You forgot to do something—that I don't believe. You don't ever do anything fun until all your chores are done."

"Well I forgot so I have to go." Rachel picked up the saddle.

"What is going on with you?" Birdie asked.

"Nothing." Rachel put the saddle on Jester. "I just forgot to do some things and I have to be going."

"Rachel O'Callahan, you stop right there and tell me what is going on with you. You have been like an old sore tail bear lately and I want to know why."

"I'm not sure I know myself, Birdie, but I do know that I shouldn't be here right now."

"And why not?"

Rachel played with the saddle to keep from looking at Birdie. "I might do something that you wouldn't understand."

"What the hell does that mean?"

"I'm not sure that I understand it myself." Rachel hoped that Birdie would just tell her to leave.

"I didn't think there was anything we couldn't talk about." Birdie stood next to the horse. "I can tell when something is bothering you, and I want to know what it is."

"No you don't," Rachel said.

"Look at me when you talk to me," Birdie insisted.

Rachel turned around, pulled Birdie close, and kissed her. After the kiss she grabbed the reins and started to lead Jester out of the clearing.

"You stop right there, Rachel O'Callahan."

Rachel stopped but didn't turn to face Birdie.

"You can't do something like that to me then leave without giving me a chance to say anything about it."

Rachel played with the reins in her hand. She knew how Birdie could be when she was mad and braced herself. "I guess you're right. I owe you that."

Birdie took the reins out of Rachel's hands. "This is what I have to say about it."

Rachel didn't know if Birdie would slap her or hit her or wallop her with something so she closed her eyes to wait for whatever it would be then opened them when she felt Birdie's lips on hers.

"That is what I have to say about it."

"I don't understand."

"I was wondering if you were ever going to get around to doing that."

"I wasn't sure...."

"If you want to talk about it you can join me over there on the blanket."

Rachel watched Birdie walk away and wondered what in the hell had just happened. She still wasn't sure about staying, but she did enjoy the kiss. She started to get on the horse then took off the saddle and put it back on the log. She walked over to the blanket but didn't sit down.

"What did you mean you were wondering when would I get around to it?"

Birdie pulled her knees up under her chin and motioned for Rachel to sit down. She sat down, pulled a blade of grass, and started nibbling on it.

"Sometimes, Rachel, you are a thick as a plank."

"I am not."

"Yes, you are. I have been trying for the last few months to get you to notice me, and I had just about given up. I told myself that if you didn't do anything today then I should just forget it."

Rachel scratched her head. "I thought you were trying to get Jacob's attention. You always seemed to be where he was."

"That's because that's where you were, you ninny."

"Well I didn't know."

"Well you do now," Birdie mocked her.

Rachel pulled another blade of grass. "What do we do now?"

"You could kiss me again, I guess."

"Yeah, I guess I could." Rachel pulled herself up on her knees. Birdie lay back on the blanket pulling Rachel on top of her. As they kissed Birdie unbuttoned Rachel's shirt. Rachel rolled onto her side.

"I can't do this."

"Huh?" Birdie sat up.

"I don't know how."

"What do you mean you don't know how?"

"I just don't, okay?"

Birdie was wondering what Rachel was talking about. "How do you know you don't know how?"

Rachel pulled a blade of grass to keep from looking at Birdie. "I...uh...tried it before and messed it up."

"You had relations with someone and you never told me?"

"I didn't want you to think less of me if I told you that I had relations before I married. That is, if I ever do get married. Now that you know I don't know how maybe I should just get on out of here."

Birdie put her hand on Rachel's arm to keep her from getting up. "I don't want you to go anywhere. I want you to tell me what you are talking about."

Rachel looked away from Birdie to keep her from seeing how embarrassed she was.

"I've been with Seth Conyers, you know, the dairyman's son." After a long pause she continued. "Pa and me took the milk cow over to the dairy last fall to get her bred with Conyers bull. After we put her in the pen with the bull Mr. Conyers and Pa went into the house for some homemade corn liquor. I stayed at the fence and Seth came up and we started talking. After a while he asked me if I had ever done it, and I said no. He said if I wanted to know how to do it then I should follow him to the barn. We went up to the loft, and he turned away from me and told me to take off my clothes. I had barely got my pants down when he shoved me back onto some hay bales and started pushing himself inside me. He was grunting and groaning something awful, then all of a sudden he stiffened up, moaned real loud, and then plopped down right on top of me. He didn't move for the longest time, and I thought he was dead. I was trying to get him off of me and trying to think of what I was going to tell Pa and Mr. Conyers when Seth all of a sudden jumped up, pulled his pants up, and left. The next thing I knew Pa was calling for me, and I hurried to get down there so we could go."

Birdie shook her head. "It's not like that, Rachel. It's not like that at all."

"I would've thought different Birdie, but I tried it again and it wasn't any better then either."

"Tell me about it."

Rachel sighed. She had dreamed a long time of being with Birdie and now here she was telling her that she didn't know squat about being intimate with another person. "Last month when we went to the auction at Fallon it was my turn to stay at the stables to keep watch on the new stock. I was reading when a man came in and introduced himself and sat down and started talking. He was nice, and after a while he asked if I was hungry, so we went to the dinner house down the road a bit. When we came back he asked if he could stay a bit and I said why not. Not too long after he started to rub my shoulders and neck, then he kissed me. The next thing I knew we were laying on the cot with him on top of me grunting and groaning like Seth, and then the third time he had to stop and put it back in I threw him off of me and told him I wasn't no goddamned rodeo pony. I threw his clothes over the wall of the stall and told him to get the hell out of there. So you see, I tried it a couple of times and I don't know how to do it."

"Why didn't you tell me?"

"What was I gonna say? I couldn't tell you that I failed not only once but twice when I tried to make love."

"No Rachel, you didn't have the right teachers was all. Making love is very beautiful with the right person."

"I wouldn't know that, now would I?" Rachel looked at Birdie. "Besides, how would you know so much about it anyway?"

"I have learned about these things too, you know."

"What?"

"I haven't told you everything either."

"When?"

"Last year."

"Last year?" Rachel asked. "Who?"

"It really doesn't matter."

"I told you who I did it with."

"Okay, it was Josiah Wellington."

"Why does that name sound familiar?" Rachel scratched her head.

Birdie pulled her legs up under her chin. "He was with the trapping party that stayed at the ranch while their leader healed from that axe wound on his leg."

"I remember the leader Jeremiah Lonegren but not anyone named Josiah."

"He drove the wagon with the supplies."

Rachel looked at Birdie with a puzzled look on her face. "You mean the one that had only one leg and the glass eye?"

"Yeah, him."

"Birdie, of all the men in the valley you mean...him?" Rachel couldn't believe what she had heard.

"Don't be so uppity about it." Birdie laughed. "He taught me a lot."

"Birdie."

"It wasn't his fault he only had one leg. He was riding on his horse at the battle of Bull Run when a cannon shell exploded right next to him. If it wasn't for the horse he might have been killed. As it was he lost his leg and one eye and other parts but managed to survive and survive quite well."

"What other parts?" Rachel asked.

Birdie scrunched up her face. "His man parts. He didn't have any man parts."

"Birdie, you're pulling my leg. You are crazy if you think I am gonna believe that."

"He really didn't have any man parts. They were blown off when the shell exploded."

Rachel folded her arms together and grunted. "So how could he make love to you if he didn't have any man parts?"

"Very well, if you want to know. He learned how to do it from his wife."

"Now I know you're making this all up." Rachel shook her head.

"I am not, and I swear by it," Birdie said, holding up one hand. "He said he was in a Union hospital and the surgeons had to cut away what was left of his mangled leg and everything else. He told them to write a letter to his wife and tell her he had been killed in battle so she wouldn't have to see him like that. To his surprise she showed up to claim the body so they had to take her to him. She put him in the wagon and took him back to Kentucky to their farm and nursed him back to health. He tried to get her to divorce him so she could get another man that could please her but she wouldn't have any of it. Over the next few years she showed him how to please her, and now he makes love to all the women he meets like that."

"Why doesn't he stay at home with his wife?" Rachel asked.

"She's dead. She got cholera and died on him about five years ago. He said he couldn't stay on the farm because he couldn't stop thinking about her, so he sold it and took up with the trappers. They needed a wagon driver and cook so he hired on and travels with them. He says the worst thing about it all is that he has to pee like a girl."

"I'm still not sure if I should believe what you are telling me," Rachel said, shaking her head.

Birdie pushed Rachel back onto the blanket and leaned over her. "First we'll take this off." She unbuttoned Rachel's shirt. "Then I'll show you how much I learned."

Rachel's grip on the blanket loosened when Birdie crawled up and lay by her side.

"That, my dear Rachel, is how you make love."

Rachel sighed. "I didn't know it was like that."

"I know," Birdie said. "I know I'll never meet Josiah's wife, but I am very thankful she showed him what she did."

"Amen to that," Rachel said.

Birdie kissed Rachel. "He taught me several ways to please a woman and this is number two."

Chapter Five

The next morning Rachel walked into the kitchen, poured herself a cup of coffee, and sat down at the table. Birdie was already sitting at the table but didn't look at her.

"You two were out late last night," Adele said when she put a plate of food in front of her. "I thought you said that you wouldn't be gone after dusk."

"I guess we didn't notice the time, Ma."

"That's no excuse, young lady. Both of you should be ashamed for worrying me like that."

"I'm sorry, Adele. It's my fault. I just got carried away and didn't want to leave, and I convinced Rachel to stay with me." Birdie kept her head down so Adele couldn't see her blush when she spoke.

"You both know how things are around here, and it isn't good for you two to be alone out there even if it is on the ranch. Maybe I should send one or two of the boys with you from now on. That way I'll know you will be back before dark and I won't have to worry."

"No, Ma, that won't be necessary. I promise." Rachel looked at Birdie. "We promise not to be late again don't we, Birdie?"

"Yes, ma'am." Birdie held up her hand.

Adele poured coffee into their cups and set the pot in the middle of the table. "I'll let it go this time, but if you are even a little bit late again I'll make the boys go with you, do you understand?"

"Yes, ma'am." They spoke in unison.

"I promised Pa that I'd help him this morning so I gotta go." Rachel finished her coffee.

"Tell your Pa that he needs to get the thrasher back from Mr. Giddings," Adele said as the door slammed shut."

"Yes, ma'am," Rachel yelled back.

"I got to look in on the mare. She is just about to drop that foal, and I want to be there when she does in case there is a problem." Birdie took her hat off of the peg on the wall.

"Birdie."

"Yes, ma'am."

"I just don't want anything to happen to you. I promised your mother I would take care of you, and if something happened to you I don't know what I would do. I can't protect you if you don't let me or help me."

Birdie hugged her. "I know, Adele, and I'll do my best from now on not to worry you any more."

Rachel grabbed Birdie's arm when she walked into the barn, pulled her behind a stack of hay bales, and kissed her.

"Rachel, stop it."

"Why?"

"Because...you can't do that here."

"Why not?"

"Somebody might see us." Birdie looked around to see if they were alone.

"So let them." Rachel tried to kiss her again.

"Rachel stop it. You're gonna get us in big trouble."

"So what are we supposed to do, just forget about it? I can't do that, not now."

"I want to be with you too, but we got to be careful about it. I've been thinking that we need some kind of signal that we can use to tell each other when we can be together."

"Like what?" Rachel shrugged her shoulders.

"I know, we'll use the bucket in the milk house. If it's hung up by the rope on the wall then the other will know to meet at the springs. If it is placed upside down on the bench then it means that we won't go. If we check everyday then we can get our chores done and meet at the springs. Okay?"

"Okay, I guess," Rachel said.

"Rachel, it's the only way we can do it." Birdie kissed her. "Now get out of here before we get carried away and do something stupid and get caught."

They spent every moment possible at the springs, believing that they would be together forever on the ranch.

Chapter Six

Sean hung his hat on a peg on the wall beside the door then sat down at the dinner table.

"Did you wash up, Sean?" Adele asked when she set a platter of food in front of him.

He held up his hands for her to see. "Yes, Mother."

Adele sat down at the other end of the table from him. "I have enough children to worry about, and I don't need another one."

After saying grace he stabbed a piece of meat from the platter. "I got a visit from the foreman of the Two Step ranch this afternoon. He told me that the fence up north has been damaged by strays. Rachel, I need you to go up there and fix it. Your ma will get some provisions ready after dinner for an early start."

"Tomorrow?" Rachel thought about the short work day she had planned. She and Birdie would be at the springs by early afternoon. "I have plans for tomorrow."

"Well I hate to change your plans, but that fence needs to be mended and it comes first. We can't stand to lose any beef, and I certainly don't want to pay for any damages caused by them cows either. It shouldn't take more than three or four days at the most anyway."

"Three or four days." Rachel looked at Birdie. "Couldn't Jacob or Joachim do it?"

"Nope, afraid not. Jacob and Alejandro are taking the threshing machine to the blacksmith for repair of that broken blade, and I promised Joachim to Mr. Hall for a few days until his help gets back from Bishop." He smiled at her. "I know you, and you'll probably be done in no time."

"Can Birdie go with me? We can get it done real fast then."

"No, I guess not. Your ma is going to need her help with the orchard picking and canning. The garden is ripe, and we can't afford to lose the food. We are stretched to the limit as far as help goes, and I can't spare anyone now."

"Pa." Rachel was upset.

"You know that once your father has his mind made up it's no use to keep talking about it," Adele said.

"Damn it." Rachel slapped the table.

Adele held up her hand. "I don't want to hear any more of that from you, young lady. I know you know better."

"Sorry Ma...Pa. I just had plans was all."

Rachel put the shovel next to the other tools in the back of the wagon. She whistled for Luke, her big black dog, then shut the tailgate after he jumped in.

Adele put a basket and small bag under the seat. "This should be more than enough, but I just want to make sure you have enough."

"You worry too much, Ma." Rachel climbed onto the wagon and sat on the seat. "See you in a few days."

Adele watched Rachel drive out of the yard, thinking about the dangers of her daughter being out by herself. She would have worried less if Birdie could go with her, but this time of year it was all they could do to get everything done before the cold weather set in.

Chapter Seven

Adele sat in the rocker on the porch with the snap peas in a bowl on her lap. She looked up when the old dog laying next to her started bark. She could tell that the riders were cavalry and put the bowl down. They stopped when the lead rider held up his hand.

"Morning to you, ma'am. I am Major Wilson." He looked around as if trying to find someone or something, then dismounted and walked to the porch. "I need to talk to your husband. Do you know where I might find him?"

"He's out in the field right now. Can I help you?"

"I really think it prudent if I talk to him, ma'am."

"We both own this ranch, so if there is anything you have to say to him you can say it to me."

The major sucked air between his teeth and tongue. He looked at the sergeant behind him and shook his head. Goddamned women, he said low enough for only the sergeant to hear.

"Ma'am, I...."

"Adele, what do you want me to do with these?" Birdie said when she walked around the corner of the house holding a basket.

"Bring them to me, then please go find Sean and bring him back as quickly as you can." She held her hand out for the basket. "You can go through the house.

"Could my men water the horses, ma'am? It's been a terrible hot ride.

"Yes."

"Sergeant, take care of the horses." The major gave his reins to the sergeant.

Sean walked around the side of the house with Birdie close behind him. "Can I help you?

"I am here on official business, Mr. O'Callahan. As a matter of fact, she is the reason I am here." He pointed at Birdie. "I have information that you have been harboring against government policy. That is a serious offense and could get you in a lot of trouble. I have to take her and any other Indians you have to the reservation."

"She is my daughter," Adele said, "and you can't take her."

"Ma'am, I don't need or want any problems, but I must tell you that I can and will take any means at my disposal to get the Indians."

"I won't let you take them."

"And what means are you talking about, major?" Sean asked.

"I have the authority to confiscate your ranch if need be."

"Sean, he can't do that, can he?" Adele asked.

"Oh yes he can, and he will," The sergeant said before Sean could speak.

"Sergeant, are the men ready?"

"Yes sir, as soon as we get the Indians. I hear tell there is her and two boys," The sergeant said.

"I will take possession of her and her brothers now." The major mounted his horse. "Bring the two boys here."

"I can't do that right now, major," Sean said.

"Mr. O'Callahan, I have been quite patient so far, so don't push me."

"The boys—her brothers—are away right now and won't be back for two days or so. One is helping a neighbor to the south and one is in town with my son to get the thrasher repaired at the blacksmith. I won't be able to get them all together until the day after tomorrow."

"Don't try any shenanigans on me, O'Callahan," The major snarled. "I will have this place torn apart if need be."

"I am not trying to argue with you, major, but that is the truth. I really can't give them to you until day after tomorrow."

"Two days it is then, O'Callahan. There'd better be her and her brothers here, or I take the ranch. Sergeant, I want you to station three men outside the front gate to the ranch. The sergeant will be back in two days for all of the Indians you have." The major slapped his thigh with his glove. "Do I make myself clear?"

Sean looked at Adele as he answered the major. "Yes major, you've made your intentions known. They will be here."

"Sean, what are we going to do?" Adele said when the soldiers left.

"I don't know, Adele, I just don't know. I'll go to town in the morning to talk with the sheriff and send a wire off to the Indian affairs office in Carson City. Maybe we can stall him for a while until we get this straightened out." He put his arm around Birdie. "We'll do any and everything to stop this, Birdie. I'll find Jacob and Alejandro and get them back here. You stay put and hope for the best."

"Adele, I won't let you lose this ranch because of us. I know my brothers, like me, appreciate what you have done for us. If it is to be then it is to be. Maybe now we will be with our mother and father."

"I hope you're right, Birdie." Adele picked up the basket and sat on the rocker. "I promised your mother I would take care of you, and I mean to do that."

"Someone has to tell Rachel," Birdie said.

"What?"

"Someone has to tell Rachel." Birdie started running to the barn. "I have to tell her."

Adele followed her.

"I can tell her when she gets back."

"No, you don't understand." Birdie put the saddle on her horse. "I have to tell her."

"Birdie, I will tell her when she gets back." Adele grabbed the reins. "If they see you riding out they may think you're running away, and we don't know what they'll do."

"I'll go out back behind the orchard then switch over to the old wagon road that leads to the north cut off. They won't see me that way." She mounted the horse. "I have to get something from the cabin first."

Chapter Eight

Rachel tamped the dirt around the post with her foot then threw the shovel into the back of the wagon. Slapping her leg, she called for Luke to jump into the wagon. She removed her hat and wiped the sweat off her forehead with a handkerchief.

"I tell you, Luke, we need to get this dirt and grit and smell off of us. I'm gonna stop at the creek and jump in to clean up, and it wouldn't be too bad an idea if you didn't do it too."

She jumped into the creek fully-clothed and washed each piece of clothing as she took them off. She threw them on top of the buck brush limbs to dry after rinsing them. The soap didn't lather much in the cold water, but it did help wash the dirt and grit off, and it smelled a lot better that the creosote she had used to waterproof the posts. At the line shack she warmed up the coffee in the stove and fried some eggs and a slab of ham. She sat one tin on the table and one on the floor. When she finished she put her tin on the floor for the dog to lick. He walked over to the table then jerked his head around to the door and barked.

Rachel opened the door to look out but didn't see anything. She shut the door and the dog barked again. She cocked the rifle, opened the door, and stepped outside.

"Who's there?"

"Rachel, it's me," Birdie said.

"Birdie, what are you doing here?" She put the rifle down.

"I came to see you." Birdie stepped from behind a tree. "I thought you could use some company."

"I thought Pa said that we were tight on help and you couldn't come."

"I just came up. I wanted... needed to see you."

Rachel walked towards her.

"No, stay there." Birdie held up her hand. "I want you to turn around."

"What for?"

"You'll see, just turn around." Birdie stepped behind the tree hoping Rachel couldn't see her.

Rachel shrugged her shoulders and turned away from her. "What's going on? Is everything okay?"

"I have to get ready."

"Ready for what?" Rachel asked.

"You'll see in a minute." Birdie walked up behind Rachel. "Now you can turn around."

Rachel looked at Birdie with a puzzled look. "Why are you wearing that buckskin dress?"

"I just thought I'd surprise you is all."

"Well I am surprised to say the least. Whooee...your mother was right about that dress fitting you real good."

When Rachel kissed her Birdie hoped Rachel wouldn't notice the tears in her eyes.

"I thought you said this dress was made for someone special."

"That's why I'm wearing it. I thought this would be the perfect time to tell you how much I love you.

"I already know how much you love me. You didn't have to put this dress on to prove it."

"Rachel, I want you to do something for me."

"What?"

"I want you to swear your love for me."

"Birdie, what's going on?"

"We are alone, and this would be the perfect time to swear our love for each other while no one can bother us.

Just me and you. Unless you don't feel the same way that I do about you."

Rachel wrapped her arms around Birdie. "Of course I feel the same way about you. It's just that you caught me cold with all of this."

Birdie put Rachel's hand on her breast. "Please."

She kissed Birdie and said, "I, Rachel O'Callahan, do swear on this day that I have always loved you Birdie and I will love you until my dying day. There will be none other in my heart but you forever."

Rachel looked at Birdie. "You have something to say?"

"I, Birdie, do swear my love for Rachel O'Callahan on this day. No matter what journeys we may take, together or apart, I will always love you. I will forever keep you in my heart."

Birdie kissed Rachel then untied the straps of the dress. "Make love to me," she said when it fell to the ground.

The interior of the shack was lit by the moonlight shining through the window. Birdie lay on her side with her head cradled on Rachel's shoulder. She could hear Rachel's heartbeat and feel the steady rhythm of her breathing. She wanted to wake her to make love again and feel her strong arms around her and the touch of her hands. She wanted to feel the tightness in Rachel's body when she was satisfied. She wanted to, but then she couldn't do what she had to do.

Gently, she ran her fingers down Rachel's cheek. Slowly, she raised Rachel's arm to get out of bed and get dressed. Kneeling next to the bed, she kissed Rachel and thought about their time together. When she opened the door to leave she wanted to look back but knew that if she did she would stay. The O'Callahans wouldn't lose the ranch because of her. Goodbye Rachel, she whispered as she shut the door.

Chapter Nine

Birdie and the three other Indian women waited for the soldier to open the gate to the compound. They had been separated from the men outside the fort with only the women being taken inside. Once inside they were shuffled into a small pen while a soldier rode his horse around the perimeter, looking at each woman while writing on a piece of paper. He stopped his horse and pointed at Birdie then ordered one of the soldiers to take her out of the pen. He circled her with the horse and smiled.

"Put her back in, soldier, and take care not to hurt her."

One of the women was talking to a soldier at the back of the pen. Birdie walked closer to listen.

"Where is my husband?" the woman asked.

"Don't you worry about that. In a few days you'll probably see him. We do this to make sure the right ones get to the reservation. Some of the men are what we call incorrigible so we make sure there isn't any trouble."

"My husband is old and not well. He is too old to be trouble for you."

"Well I guess if that's true then you'll see him soon."

"When will we go to the reservation?" the other woman asked.

"When the major gives the okay to go, I guess."

"What about my brothers?" Birdie asked. "We came from

Mason Valley and have lived on the ranch all our lives. We haven't done anything to anyone."

"Well I guess that depends on the major's mood. If he wants they will go to the pyramid reservation or they will go south."

"I've never heard of a reservation to the south."

"No reservation," the woman said. "I hear about land below ours. Mexico, I think it is called."

"You can't send them there. They don't belong there," Birdie said.

"They don't belong here either." He laughed at her and spit some tobacco at her feet. "Besides you can't stop it anyway."

The soldiers opened a gate at the rear of the pen to let Birdie and the women into a larger area. Birdie wondered how long they would be there before leaving for the reservation and wondered if Sean could get her out of the fort. She walked around the compound several times then sat on a large boulder and put her head down on her knees and started to cry.

"Cry not good." A large woman sat next to her. "Not help. Nothing change."

The gate to the compound opened to let the major pass through followed by the sergeant and several soldiers. They followed the major as he listened to the soldier who had circled the women in the pen on horseback. The soldier with the paper would talk to the major about each woman they passed, and the major would say something to the sergeant, then the woman would be taken out of the compound or left behind. They circled the compound and were almost out of the gate when the man with the paper stopped and looked back. He saw Birdie and pushed through the other women to get to her.

"This is the one I was telling you about." He pointed at Birdie.

"Stand up," the major said to her.

She didn't move.

"The major said to stand up," the sergeant said as he grabbed her arm and jerked her up. "You will do what the major wants."

The major walked around her, then stroked her hair. "I see what you mean, soldier. She will be worth a lot to us." He saluted the sergeant. "You know what to do. We will leave in the morning." He turned to leave, then stopped and looked at Birdie. "Make sure she is taken care of."

"Yes, sir." The sergeant saluted him. "You two soldiers take this list and get to parceling them women out. We ain't got a lot of time, so get with it."

The sergeant left the soldiers with the paper. The women were separated into two groups. Birdie was told to go to the back of the compound along with seventeen others. The women near the gate were taken out of the fort. Before the gate was closed, a soldier carrying a burlap sack and a bucket of water walked into the middle of the compound and put them down. "If I was you I'd eat. Tomorrow's gonna be a long day."

Birdie watched the other women scramble to get food from the sack and scoop water from the bucket with the tin cups the soldier had thrown on the ground.

"You eat." It was the old woman.

"I'm not hungry," Birdie said.

"You eat...drink." The old woman held up a piece of dried meat and a cup. Birdie took it from her and walked back to the rock and sat down. She nibbled on the meat and wondered what life would be like on a reservation.

Chapter Ten

The first rays of morning sun were shining over the eastern sky when Birdie and the other women were led out of the compound. The soldiers were on horseback with the sergeant in front, one soldier on each side of the band of women, and two following behind with rifles. Birdie walked with a young girl who had been brought into the compound late in the evening. The girl had been brought from east of Wabuska with her mother and father. The sergeant followed the road west then south as if to go to Yerington. Birdie knew the reservation was to the north of the fort.

"The reservation is north of here," she said to one of the soldiers. "We are headed south."

"You don't worry about it," the soldier answered back.

Two miles from the fort a woman sat down, refusing to go any further. Without stopping, the sergeant told one of the men to take care of the situation. The soldier on the left stopped his horse next to the woman and waited for the rest of the group to pass. Birdie stopped to talk to the woman, but the soldier put his rifle barrel on her shoulder and motioned for her to get back into the group. She wondered if he would take her back to the compound to join the women still there. They stopped momentarily to look back when they heard the gunshot. The soldier dragged the woman's body into the sagebrush.

"Anyone else want to go back to the fort?" The sergeant asked. "I didn't think so."

They stopped for the night in a dry wash. After all the women had been shackled together by their ankles one of the soldiers gave each of them a piece of dried beef and a cup of water. Birdie leaned against the bank of the wash and closed her eyes. She kept thinking about the woman who refused to go any further. She opened her eyes when one of the women yelled at a soldier after he pushed her to the ground and lay on top of her. The woman tried to kick him, and he laughed when he pulled her dress up. Birdie pushed him off of the woman. When he tried to get up she kicked him in the groin. He staggered backwards trying to draw his knife from the sheath. Birdie kicked it from his hand and picked it up. Both of them jumped when the sergeant fired a round into the dirt.

"Put it down or I shoot one right through you."

"Thanks Sarge, I'll take it from here." The soldier off brushed his clothes. He grabbed Birdie's arm.

"Leave them alone."

"Come on Sarge, let me have her."

"You take first watch tonight."

"God damn it Sarge, they's gonna git all used up anyway." The soldier kicked at the dirt. "Why can't we have a little fun with 'em?"

"Because the major cain't get what he wants if they is already used up." He jerked his head. "Go on and get out of here."

Birdie made sure the woman on the ground was all right then sat back down. The sergeant stood over her and leaned the rifle barrel on her shoulder. "Any more of that and I'll shoot first and ask about it later. You hear me?"

Chapter Eleven

Three days later they started climbing up the east side of the Sierra Nevadas. The morning of the fifth day they walked down into a valley with a lake. Birdie knew they were on the west side of the lake her mother called Dao'a aga. Her mother had taken her there several times when she was a little girl. She wondered when they would turn north to the reservation. They walked along the shoreline of the lake for two days then climbed up over a steep summit and down into a valley northwest of the lake. At the tree line above the valley floor the sergeant told the soldiers to hold the women at that spot. He rode out into the middle of the meadow, fired his rifle three times, waited a few minutes, then fired three more times. In the distance another rifle could be heard answering the sergeant. At the opposite side of the valley the major appeared and rode towards the sergeant. At the same time two riders entered the meadow from his left with a wagon following them.

"Good to see you, sir." The sergeant saluted as the major rode up to him.

"Sergeant," the major scanned the valley for the women, "how is the merchandise?"

"We lost only one sir." The sergeant pointed at the riders across the meadow.

"Who is it this time?"

"Big Jake."

"Big Jake, I thought he was dead. I heard he got into a fracas with one of them miners. He's got more lives than a god damned cat."

"Bring the women on down so we can deal," the major said.

The sergeant took a white handkerchief out of his pocket then tied it to the rifle barrel and waved it in the air. The soldiers walked the women across the meadow to where the major and sergeant were. Birdie was made to wait until all of the women had left before the soldier guarding her would let her follow. He made her stand to the side of his horse away from the rest of the group.

Big Jake circled the women on his horse. "Well, I do think you have a good looking bunch of squaws here, major. I always enjoy doing business with you cause you have a real good eye when it comes to the women."

"As much as I enjoy chatting with you, Jake, I must insist on getting this done. I have some very important business waiting for me at the fort," the major said.

"No doubt to find some more lovely merchandise."

"I wouldn't worry myself about it if I were you," the major snorted. "Sergeant, show the women up here."

The sergeant ordered the soldiers to bring seven women closer for Big Jake to look at. Big Jake motioned for a man who had been waiting in the distance behind him to join them.

"I'll be damned if it isn't you, Frenchy," the sergeant said.

"Yes ees me. I no see you here," the man motioned towards the trees, "for a long time. I meet Big Jake and geet to see old friends now."

Frenchy grabbed one of the women by the wrist and pulled her towards Big Jake.

"Twenty," the major said.

"Twenty it is," Big Jake answered back.

Birdie watched and listened as each woman was sold to Big Jake. As the group of women dwindled down she looked around for a way to escape. The young girl who had been brought to the fort after Birdie was the next to be bid on. Frenchy yelled and released his grip on her when she bit him on the wrist. She ran across the meadow, heading for the trees.

"Sergeant Crouse, take care of it," the major yelled.

The sergeant pulled his rifle out of the scabbard and fired at her. She grabbed her side and fell to the ground, then got up to run again. Birdie tried to grab the rifle to stop the second shot, but the soldier guarding her knocked her down to the ground with his rifle butt. After the second shot the woman fell to the ground.

"You geet to be old man now, sergeant. You need two to kill her." Frenchy laughed at him.

"You run on out there and we'll see who's getting old." The sergeant put the rifle back in the scabbard.

"How many left, major?" Big Jake asked.

"Two. This is a very special one."

"Major, this one is a waste of your time and mine." Big Jake looked at the large woman standing in front of him.

"Now I ain't a man that would take to a woman like this, but you know that there are some men that like getting around all that fat on a woman. She'll come in handy, just wait and see."

Big Jake scratched his beard to think then spit on the ground. "How much?"

"Ten."

"Sold." The major laughed. "Sergeant, bring the little maiden up."

Birdie tried to avoid the sergeant's grip, but he was too fast. She stumbled and fell against Big Jake's horse when he pushed her.

"Git her up here, Frenchy," he said.

Frenchy grabbed her hair and pulled her backwards. She whirled around and scratched his face. He cuffed her with the back of his hand, knocking her to the ground. The sergeant dismounted to get between them then tied her hands behind her back.

"Any damage will be assessed on you," the major said.

"Frenchy, that's enough," Big Jake said as he walked his horse around her.

The major could tell Big Jake was interested in the maiden by the way he was staring at her. He just wondered how much he would be willing to pay.

"One thousand."

Big Jake either didn't hear the major or was lost in thought because he kept circling Birdie with his horse.

Finally he stopped the horse. "How much?"

"One thousand dollars."

"One thousand?" Big Jake looked at the major. "You're crazy if you think I'm gonna pay one thousand dollars for a damned Indian squaw."

"Look her over carefully, Jake. She's high dollar and you know it. We both know you've never had one of this caliber before, and just think of the men who would pay real good money for her." The major knew how to get him to agree. "Sergeant, show him."

The sergeant grabbed Birdie's blouse and ripped it open and turned her around to face Big Jake.

"Take a good look at her, Jake. With those tits and that body she'll make more money for you than all of the others combined." The major watched Big Jake's face. "But if you don't want to make that much money I know someone else who would."

"Hold your horses and let a man think," Big Jake shot back. He pulled a leather pouch from under his shirt and counted the money he had. He knew the major was right. Men would pay good money, fat money, to get next to those tits. Hell, he'd pay to get next to them himself if she belonged to someone else. He also knew the major knew he wouldn't leave without her. "I want her, major, but I'll have to return some of them if I do."

The major wanted Big Jake to think he had the best of the deal. "Okay, which ones?"

He pointed at three of the women. "Take those three back."

Frenchy pulled the women away from the group.

The major counted the money after Big Jake threw the pouch to him. "I'll be back next spring, Jake."

"What shall I do with them, major?" the sergeant asked.

"They can't go back to the fort, sergeant," The major said as he rode away.

Big Jake watched the major ride away. "Get them ready to travel. I'll meet you in Jackson. Keep them in good shape."

Frenchy whistled to the driver of the wagon. When it stopped, he tied a rope around Birdie's waist then tied the other end to a post. After mounting his horse he held up his rifle and motioned for the other women to follow him. Birdie and the other women looked back at the three women standing next to the soldiers until the trees blocked their view of them. She wondered what would become of the women then heard gunshots. She worked at getting the rope around her waist loose as she walked next to the wagon. She started walking slower and slower when the rope loosened, then stopped while the party pulled ahead of her. She cut through the narrow part of the meadow, hoping she could get into the trees and safety. She didn't have to look back to know that Frenchy was riding hard to catch her, She could feel the pounding of the horses hooves on the ground and felt the hot breath from its nostrils on her arm, then everything went black.

When she woke she was lying in the bed of the wagon. Her feet were bound together and her hands were tied to the sides of the wagon. She jerked at the ropes, trying to get free. A woman smeared some salve on the gash in her head and wrapped a bandage around it.

"Don't try to get free," the woman said as she stepped over Birdie to get to the wagon seat. "Next time he will kill you."

"Who are you?"

"I am Nadine. I am his wife." She slapped the reins and the wagon lurched forward. "Do not go against his wishes or he will kill you."

Chapter Twelve

The sun was going down behind the mountain peak when they arrived at a camp beside a stream. Two men were waiting for them and helped Frenchy shackle the women.

"Untie the bitch and get her there." Frenchy pointed to a wheel of the wagon.

Nadine untied Birdie's hands. "Come with me."

When Birdie didn't move, Frenchy shot a round into the wood next to her head. Nadine stepped in front of the gun when Frenchy re-cocked the rifle and aimed it at her.

"She is still groggy from this morning. I will help her out." Nadine held out her hand to Birdie. "He does not like Indians, and he will kill you and leave you for the coyotes if you do not stand up. You just have to make it to Canada then you will be free."

She stood up with Nadine's help. Frenchy grabbed her arm when she hopped down from the wagon and tied her hands together. He pushed her away from the other women and made her sit down next to one of the wagon wheels. Her feet were tied together with a leather strap which was tied to a wooden stake in the ground. He wrapped another leather strap around her neck and tied it behind a spoke on the wheel.

Nadine dipped stew from a large pot in the fire pit and gave each woman a bowl with a piece of bread. Birdie pushed the bowl away when Nadine offered it.

"Don't fight. There are long days ahead, and you will need your strength."

"I don't want anything from you."

"You belong to Big Jake now." Nadine held the bowl out for her again. "All you have to do is make it to Canada."

Birdie turned her head away from Nadine.

"We go north to Canada."

"If it is north then why do we go southwest?" Birdie asked.

"You will know in a few days. Don't try to escape again or he will kill you and if he doesn't then you will wish that he did."

"Why do you help him?"

Nadine looked away. "I once had the same fire that you have. I tried to get away, but he always found me. After the last beating he left me trapped in a cave until I was near death. It is easier to do what he wants than to make him beat me. Eat this, for tomorrow will be a long day."

Frenchy lay down on a blanket next to the fire and grabbed Nadine's leg when she walked by him. His hand went up under her skirt then he pulled her down to the blanket. He ordered the man sitting by the fire to watch the women. Birdie watched them and wondered what Nadine meant about the next couple of days and what she meant about getting to Canada.

The next morning the mountain was shrouded in fog and the air was cold and damp. Birdie shivered and rubbed her legs to get them warm. One man had already started a fire and had the coffee and stew warmed when Nadine woke up. She untied Birdie and put her in the back of the wagon.

"She will walk with them," Frenchy yelled at her.

"She is still not well. You gave her a deep cut."

Frenchy grabbed a handful of Nadine's hair and yanked her head back. "I said that the Indian bitch will walk."

Nadine coughed when Frenchy let go of her hair. "She will walk."

The women were having trouble climbing the mountain as the trail became steeper. Frenchy and the two men had to dismount and lead their horses. Nadine took a different road that would eventually meet back up with them at the summit of the mountain. As they climbed higher and higher one of the women fell down several times and had to be helped up. Near the top of the mountain the woman fell down again and Birdie stopped to help her. Before she could reach the woman Frenchy pushed her aside and kicked the woman with his boot. The woman rolled several feet down the mountain before grabbing onto a manzanita bush to stop her fall. After she pulled herself up to start the climb back up to where Birdie was, Frenchy pulled his pistol from his belt and shot her. Laughing, he jammed the gun back into his belt and walked past Birdie.

Chapter Thirteen

Two days later they entered a large valley with a small settlement. Frenchy called out to the men to look at the Indian women as they walked by. The men were miners looking for gold in the California foothills. The town was Jackson, and after passing through it they stopped next to a small creek. Along the edge of the creek were eleven tents. On the hill above the creek was a large tent by itself. Big Jake stepped out of the tent when he heard Frenchy barking out orders to Nadine and the two men.

"How many we lose?"

"One." Frenchy shrugged his shoulders.

"Get them settled. I got word out, and the miners are full piss and vinegar with lots of gold and the need of a woman."

Nadine made the women line up next to the creek, then two by two she led them into the tents. She made sure that Birdie was the last and led her into a tent by herself.

"This will be yours. After supper get to sleep early. Tomorrow you start to pay for Big Jake's keep."

"I don't understand what you mean."

"You will learn tomorrow," Nadine said as she left.

At the back of the tent was a cot. Along the left wall was a small table with a commode and a wash basin with a spittoon underneath. Birdie wondered what Nadine meant about the next day.

The next morning Nadine gathered the women at the fire pit and gave each one of them a long white gown then told them to go to their tents, put them on, and wait. Birdie put the gown on the cot and peered through the flaps of the tent.

"Here, take this," Nadine said as she walked into the tent.

"What is it?" Birdie asked.

"It is a sheep's bladder. If it breaks let me know, and I will get you another one."

"I don't know what to do with it."

"Just give it to the men and they will know what to do." Nadine picked up the gown and tossed it to Birdie. "You need to put this on."

Birdie watched Nadine walk over the bridge above the creek and talk to Frenchy. Big Jake and Frenchy were sitting at a table under a large oak tree next to the bridge. On the table was a cigar box. Big Jake placed his pocketwatch on a tablet next to the box. Men were lining up behind them with money in their hands. Big Jake stood upon a tree stump. "I have been waiting for you. I have something that you been needing for some time and for some money you can use my goods for some time. Let's not waste any more time, gentlemen. I am open for business."

Chapter Fourteen

Birdie watched Big Jake take money from the men and write on a tablet then point to one of the tents. She had to escape but knew that she would be seen as soon as she walked out of the tent. She jumped when the flap on the tent opened and a man walked in. He stood in the doorway looking at her.

"Well lordy, you surely are an Indian princess." He unbuttoned his pants and let them fall to the ground. "You don't have to worry none, little princess, cause I ain't gonna hurt you." When he reached for her she backed into the back wall of the tent then ducked under his arm to avoid his grasp. He grabbed her blouse and pushed her onto the cot. "I got money on you, and I'm gonna get my use."

She kicked him in the groin when he tried to get on top of her. He doubled over trying to get his breath, fell off the bed, grabbed his clothes, and crawled out of the tent. Before she could run out of the tent Frenchy threw back the flap and stepped inside, knocking her backwards onto the cot. He reached down to grab her blouse, but she kicked his arm and ran to the doorway. He spun around to grab her arm, but she jerked it away from him then he grabbed her hair. She grabbed the chair and swung it around hitting him on the side of his head when he pulled her back to him. He grabbed a leg and yanked it towards him. The motion caught her off guard and she stumbled. His fist smashed into her jaw, knocking her backwards into the desk then onto the ground. Before she could get up he landed on top of her and pinned her head down with this forearm at her throat. She struggled until he pulled his knife out of the sheath. Pressing the tip of the knife into her skin just above her knee, he pulled it slowly up the inside of her leg adding more pressure as the knife neared the top of her leg. She tried to scream, but he covered her mouth with his hand.

"I gut you like feesh and leave your entrails for the coyote." He wiped the blood from the knife on her blouse. "Now do what is told you."

He walked out of the tent and called Nadine. Birdie was still lying on the ground when Nadine walked into the tent.

"You must get up, you have work to do." She helped Birdie get up and walked her over to the cot.

"Nadine, get her ready," Big Jake yelled.

"You must get up, you have work to do," Nadine said. She picked up the gown off the ground. "The men like you to wear this." She ripped some material from the blouse and wrapped it around Birdie's leg.

"Raise your arms." Nadine undressed her and slipped the gown over her head. The blood had soaked through the bandage, but Nadine didn't seem to care. After putting everything in order she left. Soon another man entered the tent. She lay back on the cot and waited for him.

Chapter Fifteen

Three days later they left the Jackson mining district heading north following the gold camps and towns. At Sutter Creek they stayed four days then on to Hang Town. In larger towns like Hang Town they left only after the men and money played out then continued on to Coloma, Michigan Hill, and Auburn. After two weeks in the Auburn district they packed up for Grass Valley and the Empire Mining district. Whenever they moved Big Jake would leave two days before to scout out a clearing for their next camp and to announce the arrival of the women in advance. The days turned to weeks then months. Birdie learned that men wanted their satisfaction in different ways, and if she refused Frenchy would come in with a belt or his fists.

Continuing north along the Sacramento River they left the gold mining towns for the lumber towns and mills. A week was spent at Oroville with lumbermen who liked to be satisfied much the same way as the miners with the same smell of bad breath, rotting teeth, and cheap whiskey. They also reeked of pine from the pitch that had hardened on their clothes and skin that chaffed and rubbed the skin raw when they were with a woman.

Nadine woke everyone up earlier than usual one morning to get an early start for Corning in northern California. It would take four long days to get there, and they left as the sun was beginning to peak over the mountains. Birdie walked away from the women and stood behind a big pine tree. After vomiting, she felt dizzy and leaned against the tree until her head cleared then slowly followed the group. She had been sick the last few days and didn't want anyone to know. She was afraid of what Frenchy would do to her if she couldn't see the men. She lagged behind most of the time hoping he wouldn't notice.

At the camp near Corning, after refusing to eat dinner, Birdie went to her tent and lay on the cot. She closed her eyes and tried to sleep as she thought about Rachel and the ranch. If she thought about Rachel then everything she had to do was bearable. She wondered if she would ever see Rachel again.

Nadine came into the tent. "I thought you'd like some of this."

"I don't want anything." Birdie turned away from her.

"You don't look good, and this will help you feel better." She offered the cup to Birdie. "It's tea and it will settle your stomach."

"I can take care of myself."

"I don't want to get Frenchy in here."

It was very bitter, and she had trouble swallowing it. "Please leave me alone."

Nadine took the cup and left.

"Did she drink it?" Frenchy asked.

"Yes, it shouldn't be too long now." Nadine looked at the tent.

Birdie felt a sharp pain and rolled onto her side. Another jolt of pain shot through her body when she tried to stand up. She screamed and fell against the table then blacked out. Nadine and Frenchy picked her up and pulled the chair closer to her.

"Stand here and hold on to the back of the chair." Nadine said as she turned the chair around. Birdie grabbed the chair and vomited. Nadine took Frenchy's knife from the sheath and cut the waistband on Birdie's skirt, kicking it away as it fell to the ground. Birdie tried to stop the heaving in her abdomen, but everytime she tried the pain was too intense. She started gasping for breath and saw blood running down her legs, then she screamed in pain as a large mass fell onto the ground. There was another sharp pain then she blacked out.

"Watch her." Nadine left the tent and returned with a bucket of warm water. "Help me put her on the cot."

"I want her ready for tomorrow," Frenchy said.

"Not after this. You can't be serious."

"I want her ready, you hear me?" He grabbed a handful of her hair. "If she's not then you'll answer to me."

"She'll be ready.

Four days later the morning air was beginning to take on the chill of autumn. They packed up and followed Big Jake on their trek to Canada following the Sacramento River turning to the northeast at Mount Shasta. Two weeks later they camped alongside the Klamath River one mile away from Fort Klamath. The commander told Big Jake not to bring the women any closer. It just made the soldiers and lumbermen more determined to get to the women. Two weeks later Big Jake told Frenchy and Nadine to get ready to move on up north.

After the last man had left Birdie's tent she walked into the river and washed herself several times, trying to get rid of the feel and smell of the men. After dressing she lay on a large stump to warm up in the sunshine. She was nearly asleep when the screams of one of the women woke her up. Frenchy shoved a woman out of a tent and kicked her and hit her several times with his belt. The woman tried to get away from him, but he continued to hit her. Birdie jumped off the stump and grabbed a dead tree branch. She struck Frenchy in the back of his legs when he raised his belt to hit the woman again. She tried to hit him after he fell to the ground, but he rolled away from her.

"You think you can fight Frenchy?" he said as he regained his feet. "I show you how to fight." She stepped back and hit him across his back when he lunged for her. He cursed and spun around, grabbing for the branch. The second time he lunged at her she swung the branch but he ducked and grabbed a handful of hair and pulled her back to him. She jammed the branch into his stomach and started to run, but he tripped her with his foot. She dropped the branch when she stumbled. He pulled his knife out of the sheath when she reached down to pick up the branch. Weaving back and forth and tossing the knife from hand to hand he said, "I gut you like feesh and leave entrails for the Coyote."

She swung the branch and hit his arm when he lunged at her. He yelled out in pain but didn't drop the knife. He tried to circle around her, but she stayed in front of him. She tripped on a rock and stumbled backward. He charged at her, swinging the knife, but she used the branch as a shield. He picked up the belt and wrapped it once around his hand. She held up the branch when he lunged forward then he wrapped the belt around her leg and pulled on it. She stumbled toward him and he swung the knife up across her body. She cried out as the blade cut into her skin. The motion of his arm turned him around, and she hit the side of his head. He dropped the knife and she reached for it. He shoved his shoulder into her body, knocking her to the ground. He grabbed her legs to pull her back to him then straddled her. He laughed as his hands gripped her throat. She fought to keep her breath, but his grip was strong and she started to lose consciousness. She could feel herself going deeper and deeper into the darkness when his right hand eased up. He tried to pry her hands away from the knife that was buried deep in his chest. His left hand still had a strong hold on her throat, but she knew she had to keep both hands on the knife. Blood started to trickle out of the right side of his mouth when he released his grip on her throat. He started to claw furiously at her hands trying to get them away from the knife. His hands dropped down to his sides.

"I gut you like feesh..." His head dropped down to his chest. She held the knife for a few minutes more then used what strength she had left to pull her legs from underneath him before he fell backwards. She watched him for any sign of movement. She felt a sharp pain in her chest when she tried to stand up. The knife had done its job cutting her from below her right hip up across her chest slicing through her left breast

Nadine looked at Frenchy. "He's dead."

She ripped Birdie's shirt open to look at the wound. "He cut you real bad." She said to the other women, "Get over to the wagon and get me some whiskey and a large knife. Help me carry her over close to the fire. One of you, get that bucket there and get me some mud. Make sure it is good clean mud, nothing but mud."

Nadine put some logs onto the fire to build it up. When the flames died down into red hot coals she shoved the knife blade into them. She ripped some rags into long pieces, braided them together, and tied the ends together. She held up Birdie's head three times and made her swallow the whiskey. "Bite down on this." She put the braided rags in Birdie's mouth. "I want four of you to hold her arms and legs down."

The knife blade was red hot when she took it out of the coals. "Keep a real good grip on her." She pinched the wound together and pressed the blade on Birdie's skin to seal the wound. Birdie's screams were muffled by the rags. She smelled the burning flesh then passed out.

Nadine worked quickly, searing the wound with the knife, then packed the mud on top of it. Big Jake stood at the front of his tent watching the women around the fire wondering what was going on. He stood over Nadine as she finished with Birdie.

"She do that?" He pointed at Frenchy.

"Yes."

"She gonna be all right?"

Nadine finished packing the mud. "I don't know."

"We'll be leaving for Chemult tomorrow. Will she be ready?"

"I don't know." Nadine growled at him.

He pulled the knife out of Frenchy's chest. "Been wanting this for a long time now. He won't need it anymore." Wiping the blood off on Frenchy's shirt he looked back at Birdie and went back to his tent.

Nadine told one of the women to stay with Birdie while the rest of them started to pack. It would be easier in the morning to get started. The sun disappeared behind the mountain when Nadine sat next to Birdie. She thought about how much she had been like Birdie in her younger days. The fire and spunk she had were taken away by Frenchy. Why couldn't she face Frenchy like that? Even if she had been killed it would have been better than living in this hellish nightmare.

The morning fog was heavy as the women finished packing the wagon. Big Jake looked at Birdie in the wagon.

"Take her out."

"What?"

"I said take her out. She'll slow us down."

"We can't leave her, she'll die. She'll die without anyone to care for her."

"She should have thought about that before she took on Frenchy. We don't have time to be a nursemaid to a goddamned Indian."

He pulled the knife out of the sheath and jumped into the wagon when Nadine didn't move. "I'll make sure you don't have to worry about her."

"No." Nadine pulled the knife away from Birdie's throat. "We'll get her out." Three women helped her lift Birdie out of the wagon. She looked back from the seat of the wagon as it pulled away and Birdie disappeared into the fog.

Chapter Sixteen

Rachel drove the wagon up to the back porch. "Hey Ma, I got done a little early so I thought that you and me and Birdie could go into town tomorrow. If I remember right your social club is due to meet so I figured that Birdie and I could sell the eggs and canned goods while you visited."

Before Adele could answer her Rachel drove off. She followed Rachel into the barn. "Rachel, what are you talking about?"

Rachel unhooked the horses and led them into a stall. "You know that the third week of every month you go and meet with your social club. I thought the three of us could go to town and..."

Adele interrupted her. "Rachel, you know that Birdie is not here."

"She's not, where'd she go?"

"She didn't tell you?"

Rachel could tell by her mother's voice that something was wrong. "Tell me what?"

"She was supposed to tell you when she went out to the line shack."

"Tell me what?"

"The soldiers came for them two days ago."

Rachel grabbed the side of the wagon to steady herself. That's why Birdie was so insistent about the two of them swearing their love for each other.

"Why didn't she tell me?"

"I don't know Rachel. That's what she told me when she went out there."

"How long have they been gone? We'll go get them and bring them back."

"We can't."

"And why the hell not?"

"Major Wilson said if we tried to stop them he would put a lien on the ranch. We didn't have any choice."

"Son of a bitch," Rachel yelled and threw the creosote bucket against the wall.

"What in tarnation is going on in here?" Sean said when he walked into the barn. "Sounds like one of the bulls got loose or something."

"Birdie didn't tell Rachel they were being taken to the reservation," Adele said.

"You didn't try to stop them, Pa?"

"I couldn't, girl, they would've taken the ranch. I sent a telegram to the Indian agent and to the governor. I expect an answer any time now."

"That's all..." Rachel threw up her arms. "You should have gone after them. Well, I am going after them and bring them back."

"No you're not, young lady. You are not going anywhere," Sean yelled at her. "I am not going to lose this ranch because of you."

"You always said they were like your own children like Jacob and me."

"They are as much my children as you and Jacob," Adele said. "Birdie was the one who told us not to do anything. She said she didn't want us to lose the ranch because of them. She said maybe they could be with Little Bird and Joachim on the reservation."

Sean put his hand on Rachel's shoulder. "I know it's hard, girl, but someday you will meet another nice young man. I know how much you thought of Joachim, but there are plenty of good young men in the valley." He walked out of the barn shaking his head. "Sorry, honey."

Rachel sat on the tailgate and watched him walk out of the barn. She knew he was right, but there had to be something that could be done.

Adele sat in the tailgate. "I know he means well, Rachel, so why don't we just let him keep thinking that about you and Joachim."

"What?" Rachel looked at her mother. "What are you talking about?"

"Rachel, I know all about the milk house and the bucket, and I know why you two didn't want the boys at the springs. After all, I am you're mother. I just wish that Birdie had told you about this when she went to the line shack. I just wish it would have been different for your sake."

"She didn't say anything about leaving...nothing...she didn't say nothing at all."

"I'm really sorry, honey." Adele hopped down from the tailgate. "I suspect that you will want to be by yourself for a while."

Rachel watched Adele walk across the yard to the house. She thought about what she had said to Birdie and Birdie had said to her. Why didn't she notice something was wrong? Why didn't she make Birdie tell her why it was so important to swear their love for each other? She thought about their making love in the line shack and how sweet and tender it was. She wondered if they would ever make love again.

She walked to the front of the wagon, opened the wooden box underneath the seat, and removed the buckskin dress. At the door of Birdie's cabin she stopped momentarily as if expecting Birdie to come out of it. Inside the cabin she opened the hope chest and laid the dress inside and slowly closed the lid. She wanted to leave but couldn't. She wanted Birdie to be there, but she wasn't. She wanted to yell and scream, but she couldn't so she sat on the floor and cried.

Chapter Seventeen

Rachel put the packages from the mercantile in the rear of the wagon then rode to the blacksmith. She walked into the shop and watched the embers fly up from the fire pit when he squeezed the bellows.

"Hey Gus, how is the baler coming along?"

He slapped a piece of red hot iron onto an anvil then started to pound on it with a sledge hammer.

"Hey Gus!" she yelled.

"What?" He stopped pounding when he saw her.

"The baler, when is it to be ready?"

"Tell your pa I should have it ready in two days. The spindle is giving me a bit of a fit but nothing I cain't handle."

"Okay." She waved at him and left. She took the main road home to the ranch again and not across the shortcut like she used to do since Birdie had been gone. The shortcut followed the old railroad bed that crossed the one to the springs. She didn't go to the springs anymore, and the road would only remind her of them. She also didn't go into the milk house either. Her mother, without saying anything to her, started to do the milk separation for the cheese and whey. Rachel wondered when her mother knew about her and Birdie and why she never said anything about it. She saw a rider coming towards her waving his arm to get her to stop.

"Rachel, you must take my horse and get to the ranch. I

will take the wagon."

"What's wrong, Pete?"

"Something's happened to your pa and brother. They are hurt real bad. Your ma says to come and get you pronto. Take my horse, and I'll get the wagon back."

Arturo the foreman was sitting on the top step of the porch. He had a bandage on his right arm covered with blood.

"Arturo, what's going on?"

"Your father and brother is hurt real bad." He opened the door. "You should better go see them."

She ran up the stairs. "Ma!"

"I'm in here Rachel." Adele said.

She stopped at the doorway to her parents' room and saw her father lying on the bed. His left arm was turned at an odd angle, and one leg was swollen twice the size it should have been. The right side of his chest was crushed inward, and his face was cut and swollen. Adele walked out of her brother's room.

"Ma, what's going on?"

"Your father was trying to get the bull into the loading chute from the pen when he fell and got trapped in the chute. The bull trampled him and Jacob tried to help but his foot got caught and before he could get free the bull gored him. Arturo managed to get the bull out and away from them but he got hurt, too."

"How's Jacob?"

Rachel could tell by the look in her mother's eyes that it wasn't good. She stood in the doorway of his room.

"How is he, Doc?" she asked.

"I wish I could say something good, Rachel, but he's lost a lot of blood. I sewed him up as best I could. The horn cut clean through his lower belly. It doesn't look real good." He closed his bag. "I have to go see to your father."

"Come on, Jacob, you got to make it." She sat on the edge of his bed. His breathing was shallow and raspy. She brushed some hair from his forehead and held his hand. "You can't leave me with this ranch by myself."

"Rachel, you need to go see your father." Adele sat on the other side of the bed.

Rachel walked across the hall. The doctor stood at the foot of the bed. "If you want to say goodbye then you should do it now."

"No...no you don't mean that."

He went to Jacob's room.

She sat on the bed. "Pa, you got to be all right. Me and Ma we need you and Jacob, you hear me?"

The doctor walked back into the room. "Rachel, you're brother's gone."

She walked into Jacob's room and held her mother while she cried. "Ma, I'll stay with Jacob. Why don't you go see to Pa?"

She heard the loud cry from her mother and knew that her father was gone too.

The snow started to fall as the preacher gave the final words at the gravesite. Rachel stood next to her mother, not looking at the caskets but at the Sierras. She didn't realize the service was over until Mrs. Baxter gave her a hug and said she was so very sorry about what all had happened. After the last person had spoken to them she asked the preacher to walk Adele to the buggy. The wind blew harder and the snow was getting heavier. She dropped a sage branch on each casket.

"I'm sorry to hear about your father and brother." Two men were standing across the graves from her. "They were good men and we need good men to keep the settlement in the valley."

She turned to walk away.

"Uh Miss O'Callahan, I am Major Wilson and this is Sergeant Crouse, and although I realize it may not be appropriate to bring this up at this time that is a mighty big ranch for two women to handle. I am offering my services to you and your mother. It would be a lot easier on the both of you if you had a man around to handle things."

Rachel didn't have to answer him. The look in her eyes said everything she needed to say.

"I hope you know what you're doing. You can contact me at the fort if...when you need me. I bid you a good day."

She waited until they were out of the cemetery before going to the buggy.

She looked one more time at the graves and thought that it was a perfect day for a funeral. Not only did she bury her father and brother, but she knew she would never see Birdie again.

Chapter Eighteen

Rachel and Arturo stopped their horses when he spotted the cow in the ditch giving birth. They waited to make sure the cow had a good birth then watched as the newborn stood upon its legs. Rachel took a piece of paper from her pocket and added one more calf to the number of viable livestock on the ranch. It had been a good year for the calving even though the winter had been unusually cold. Ice and snow built up everywhere. Every day they worked the canals and water through to break the ice for the cattle. The winter alfalfa and hay supply had dwindled down to almost nothing, and she was glad the days were getting somewhat warmer so the grass could think about growing.

She wondered what her father would say about the number of newborn calves and what he would do to stretch the feed. Arturo pointed to a coyote walking across the meadow in front of them and drew his rifle to shoot it.

"Not today, Arturo." Rachel put her hand on the barrel of the gun. It had been four months since the accident, and she wasn't ready to see any more death. "That should do it I guess. Let's get back to the house."

"How did we do with the count?" Adele asked when Rachel walked into the kitchen.

"We're gonna have a good bunch."

"I wish your dad and Jacob could see that. It seems funny

that would happen after..." Tears came to Adele's eyes.

Rachel didn't answer because she knew it would only upset her mother even more. They dealt with the deaths in their own ways, and she knew that spring would be especially hard on her mother. This would be the first spring that she and her father wouldn't go to Virginia City for a little time together by themselves. It would be the start of a lot of things that were taken for granted that they would have to deal with as time passed by.

"Ma, why don't you sit down and rest for a while?"

"I'm not tired. Besides I have to get the eggs, the hens have been laying a lot lately." She wiped her hands on her apron and picked up an envelope. "Mrs. Culbertson's letter said she would be by this week with the money from the miners in Rawhide. I think we can give her six dozen or so. Arturo said he can give three cans of milk also, so we should have quite a lot of money in the box."

The box in the cupboard was where the money was kept from selling the eggs and milk. Her parents used it to give themselves a treat, and it was never to be used for the ranch. In Virginia City Adele would buy a new hat and dress for church and Sean would get a new pair of pants and a shirt from the Sears and Roebuck catalog.

The would see a play at the Piper's Opera House then have a good fancy dinner at the Delta Saloon followed by dancing. The Territorial Enterprise newspaper was always posted in the window of the mercantile with a list of the upcoming events around Virginia City in the spring edition. Rachel tried to think of ways to keep her mother from reading it when they went into Yerington town the next day.

Adele stopped on the top step of the Smythe mercantile building to talk to a friend while Rachel continued inside. She saw Mrs. Perot at the back in the dry goods section.

"Morning, Mrs. Perot."

"Good morning, Rachel. How are you and your mother doing these days? It was such a loss of your father and brother."

"We are doing best we can, I guess. That's why I am here right now. I need to know if the Sears catalog has arrived yet."

"Yes, it has. It's right back there on the counter. Is there something you want to order from it?"

"No, I thought it might be a bit hard for Ma to see it. You know she and Pa would always buy his new pants and shirt before they went to Virginia City. If she asks would you tell her that it hasn't come yet?"

"Maggie, don't listen to her. She is becoming like an old mother hen. If you have the catalog I would like to see it please."

"Ma, I don't think it's good for you to look at."

"Rachel, I can't live my life in the past, and I suspect that you're father wouldn't want that either. I will continue to read that catalog as long as I am alive, no matter the circumstances."

"Yes ma'am," Rachel said.

"Now I know you want to protect me, but I am a grown woman and I can take care of myself. Mrs. Perot has the catalog arrived yet?"

"Yes it has, Adele." Mrs. Perot walked to the back of the store. "I also got a catalog from a new dress pattern company if you want to look at it."

"I most certainly would."

Placing the catalogs on the counter Mrs. Perot opened the dress pattern catalog to a dog eared page and pointed at a dress. "I was looking at this one. It looked quite daring and scandalous."

"My yes, it is," Adele said. "How much material would it take?"

Rachel listened to her mother and Mrs. Perot and smiled to herself. She walked around the store looking for Sedwick the clerk. He was stacking boxes on the top shelf.

"Hey Sedwick, I have a list of things from Ma."

"Okay, Rachel, I'll get to them as soon as I get these boxes in order. Just put it on the counter."

"Okay." She took a piece of licorice out of a jar. "Put this on the bill too, okay?"

"Uh-huh."

She sat in a chair outside the doors to wait for her mother. Several people stopped to give condolences about her father and brother and to ask how she and Adele were doing. Several waved as they passed by on horseback or wagons. Some offered help when it came time to cut the alfalfa. She leaned back on the back legs of the chair and closed her eyes.

"Miss O'Callahan, it's nice to see you. I have been wondering how you and your mother are doing."

She opened her eyes to see Major Wilson standing next to the chair.

"We are doing just fine." She didn't like him, and she didn't know why but there was something about him that rankled her nerves.

"Remember that I'm always available to help."

She set the chair down on all four legs. "We don't need…."

"Oh there you are," Adele said when she walked out of the store. "I am ready to go now. Mrs. Perot and I have had quite a nice chat, and I picked out some new patterns to sew. Sedwick has the order filled so would you be a dear girl and go bring it to the wagon?"

Rachel pushed her way past the major. "I'll get the basket."

"We need to go by the doctor's house to give them some eggs then we can get back to the ranch," Adele said when Rachel sat on the seat.

"It's going to be late when we get home so I thought maybe we could stop at Clancy's dinner house and eat."

Adele wrapped her arm around Rachel's. "That would be nice."

Chapter Nineteen

Summer took its time arriving, but Rachel didn't mind. It had been quite a few years since spring lasted long enough for all of the desert flowers to bloom and the fruit trees to get blossoms past the last hard frost. This year they would have plenty of fruit to can and pack away for the winter. The snow on the Sierras kept the afternoon breeze cool all summer and the cattle fattened up on the lush valley grass. Four cuttings of alfalfa would help with the coming winter's feed for the ranch as well as making a profit when she sold it and the cattle to Fort Lyon, their biggest buyer, for their stockade.

She checked to make sure all the provisions were in place for the drive north to the fort. Her mother told her not to worry about the ranch as it would be there when she got back. Arturo would lead, Rachel would be at the end, and the rest of the hands would keep the herd together. Carmeta, Arturo's wife, would drive the chuck wagon and keep everyone fed during the three day ride. Rachel closed the gate and waved goodbye to her mother.

A mile from the fort Arturo stopped the herd and waited for Rachel to join him. They rode ahead of the herd to make arrangements for the delivery. They stopped at the gate while a soldier notified the commandant they were there. The soldier led them into the purser's room and left. Rachel walked around the room, looking at the maps and pictures on the walls. She looked at the new map of the United States with two new states and territories.

"Miss O'Callahan, it's nice to see you again." Major Wilson held out his hand.

Rachel shook his hand but didn't like the way it felt. It was not at all like her father's strong and steady grip.

"It's been a while since I have been here."

"You've been here before?" The major seemed surprised. "That must have been quite a while ago as I have been here for a few years now. It's not often we get the pleasure of a woman's company here in the fort. Especially someone as lovely as you."

Rachel ignored the remark. "I brought your cattle for the fort. You know, of course, that the government has bought our cattle for years now and I am here with this year's herd."

The major sat in a chair behind a desk and leaned back onto two legs. "I guess you didn't get the letter."

"What letter?" Rachel asked.

The major scratched his beard. "I sent you a letter telling you that we can't buy your cattle."

"Why?" Rachel was wondering what was going on.

He put his feet upon the desk. "Your herd has been quarantined."

"What? Since when has my herd been quarantined? I've been selling my cattle for weeks to all of my regular buyers and not one has mentioned quarantine. Not even the brand inspectors." She slammed her fist on the desk. "Who the hell put the quarantine on my cattle?"

"It will do no good to get angry, Miss O'Callahan. I must abide by the order of the quarantine and not have any of your cattle here at the fort."

"What the hell am I going to do with them? I can't keep them all winter, and it's too late to drive them anywhere else to get a good price for them."

"That's not my concern, is it? Whatever you do with them is now your problem."

"Son of a bitch." She jerked the door open. "Let's go,

Arturo."

"How did she take it?" Sergeant Crouse came into the room after she left.

"Just like I thought. By the time she gets anyone to buy them the market price will be rock bottom." The major rolled a cigarette. "With those cows eating all the winter feed before the season is out and with her account on hold at the mercantile it shouldn't take long for that ranch to be in trouble. I'll make myself available to them when the time is right." He blew a smoke ring. "I can't live on an army pension and that ranch would be all I need."

Four days later Rachel sat at the desk where her father kept his business papers. She had looked in every drawer twice and couldn't find a letter from the army about the quarantine. She ran her fingers through her hair then slammed her fist on the desk.

"Rachel, it's not going to help anything to get upset," Adele said.

"What can I do but get upset, Ma? I can't find no letter from the cavalry about any quarantine."

"Maybe he was mistaken. Maybe he just got things mixed up."

"Well it's a damned big mistake, I'll say. I got cattle to feed that should have been gone, and I don't have enough feed to get them all through the winter. We'll be digging trenches from here to kingdom come to bury the carcasses."

"Adele?" Carmeta stood at the doorway to the room.

"What is it, Carmeta?"

"I try to get supplies you ask for at the mercantile. They tell me that you have no credit no more. It has been stopped."

"What?" Rachel said.

"Mrs. Perot say that a letter she got told her to stop your credit and not to sell you anything unless it is money in hand."

"Jesus Christ." Rachel slapped the desk.

"Rachel, calm down."

"Calm down?" Rachel paced around the room. "First I can't sell the cattle and now we can't buy from the mercantile unless we have cash, and we can't get cash unless we sell the cattle. Why the hell should I calm down?"

"Because it doesn't do any good to get mad." Adele opened the top of the desk. "We need to think of a way to get around this for now then find out what is going on. I want you to go to Virginia City tomorrow and get us an attorney. I have the name of one that was given to me by Bertha Higgins last year when she visited me after the funeral." She shuffled through some papers.

"Here it is."

"I don't know anything about talking to no attorney."

"You have to do it."

"Why me?"

"Because if you don't we could lose the ranch. Your father and I spent an entire lifetime so we could give it to you and Jacob. Things have turned so you are the caretaker now, and it is up to you to do it."

Rachel took the paper. "I'll leave in the morning."

Chapter Twenty

Rachel pulled the collar of her coat up to keep the wind from blowing down the back of her neck as she rode into Yerington. She left Jester at the livery stable then bought a ticket to Virginia City from the ticket agent. The train stopped briefly at Carson City then slowly wound its way up Sun Mountain to Virginia City. She thought of the two times she had been in Virginia City. One time was with her family for a Fourth of July celebration and the other was when her mother and the other women of the quilting society were visiting to raise money for the orphaned children's home of Carson City. She wondered if the front of the train would hit the caboose as it almost made a complete circle to the left then it turned to the right to climb another hill and turn back into it. The train struggled around the curves and up the mountain, but finally it stopped at the depot.

    At the station she asked the telegraph clerk for a hotel. He pointed to a building on D Street called **Miss Mabelle's Inn**. After signing the register, she paid for a room and a bath. She liked riding the train, but she wanted to wash off the soot and ash from the smoke stack. She asked about something to eat, but all they had was a slice of ham and one boiled egg as the cook had gone home for the evening.

    The next morning she asked the waitress in the dining hall where B Street was and had she ever heard of an attorney named Thadeus C. Mathews. The waitress had never heard of Thadeus C. Mathews but told her if she walked out the back door down the stairs to the street below the hotel and headed north to the end of the street she could find the address. The last building was a small mercantile with the office of Thadeus C. Mathews, Attorney at Law, on the top floor. She walked up the narrow flight of stairs and knocked on the door.

"Enter," a voice shouted from inside the room.

She reached for the knob then the door opened.

"Come, come." A man waved his hand at her to enter the room. "I don't want any of the spice to get out."

A large bowl on a small table was filled with hot water and several different kinds of flower petals. He picked up a small stick and stirred the mixture in the bowl. "Smells like heaven doesn't it?"

"Hmm," Rachel said.

"Supposed to relieve tension and make one at ease. At least that's what the Chinese lady at the joss house told me." He took a deep breath then walked over to the window and raised it about an inch.

"I am Thadeus C. Mathews, ma'am, and I welcome you to my office." He put on a black suit coat and sat in a chair behind a desk. "What, may I ask, is your reason for being here to see me?"

"I am Rachel O'Callahan, owner of a ranch in Mason Valley...."

Before she could finish what she was saying he jumped up from the chair to look at a map of the state of Nevada on the wall behind the desk.

"Mason Valley...." He pointed at the map. "Where is Mason Valley?"

Rachel wondered if she was wasting her time with him if he didn't know where Mason Valley was.

"I am sorry, Miss...."

"Rachel O'Callahan."

"Thank you." He smiled at her. "I have been here seven

months, and I've just gotten the hang of the lay of the land around here and Carson City, so please bear with me."

She walked to the map on the wall and tapped it with her finger. "This is Mason Valley and this is Yerington. Half a day's ride by train from here. One on horseback. I live a few miles outside of town to the southwest a bit." She walked to the door. "I am sorry to have bothered you."

"Please, Miss O'Callahan, I am asking you for your patience."

"I don't know." She turned the door knob.

"Why not? You're already here."

He was right that she was already in his office, so what would it hurt to talk to him? She would just have to find another attorney and not knowing anyone in Virginia City it could take another day or so and she needed to get back to the ranch.

"I have to talk to someone about my ranch and my cattle and the quarantine. I need to get some help or I could lose my ranch. I need someone that knows about this kind of stuff, and you don't seem to fit the bill."

"Please don't leave." He pushed a straight-backed chair to his desk and motioned for her to sit. "I may be relatively new to Virginia City, but I need you as much as you need me, so please tell me what you're problem is."

She sat in the chair. "For years my pa sold the cattle from our ranch to Fort Lyon. I have the ranch now, and when I drove the cattle to the fort I was told that my herd had been quarantined and they wouldn't buy them. I can't keep...."

He interrupted her. "Were you given a reason why the cattle were quarantined?"

She wondered if he always interrupted people that were talking. "No."

"You can't keep...?" He asked her.

"Keep what?" She answered him.

"I don't know, Miss O'Callahan, you said that you can't keep them then you stopped."

"That's because you didn't let me finish."

"Sorry." He stirred the contents of the bowl. "Please go on."

"I can't keep all the cattle through the winter because I don't have enough feed for all of them. I have only enough feed for the breeders and the selected bulls. Major Wilson at the fort said his superiors told him not to take the herd. He said a letter was sent to me, but I never got one from the government, the brand inspector, or anyone else about any quarantine. If I don't sell them I will lose the ranch."

"Who told you about the quarantine?"

"Major Wilson at the fort."

"Are you sure that you didn't get a letter from the government?"

"Yeah," Rachel growled at him.

"I'm not disputing what you are saying, Miss O'Callahan, but I need to make sure that you don't know why all this is taking place." He turned his chair around and looked at the bookcase behind the desk. He took a book from the shelf, thumbed through it, and marked a page with a dog ear. "Why don't you go on home and I will see what I can find out?"

"Maybe you didn't hear me right. Mason Valley is a day's ride south of here."

"I heard you, Miss O'Callahan."

"I don't have a lot of time to wait, Mr. Mathews. South is the only way I can drive my herd to sell them and the longer I wait the lower the price will be when or if I can sell them."

"I will notify you of my progress. Now go home and don't worry."

Didn't see too many women like her in Sacramento, he thought as he stood at the window watching her walk up the street. He sat in his chair and opened the book.

Chapter Twenty-one

Two days later Thadeus Mathews stopped his buggy next to the porch of the main house of the ranch. He walked up the stairs and knocked on the screen door.

"May I help you?" Adele asked him.

"Hello, my name is Thadeus Mathews, and I am looking for Miss Rachel O'Callahan."

"She is out back mowing the field right now."

"Uh huh." He took a handkerchief from a pocket and wiped his forehead. "Well I guess I'll have to wait."

"Would you like to sit on the porch while you wait?"

"That would be nice, thank you." He sat in a rocker. "The shade helps."

"Would you like some lemonade? I made some fresh this morning."

"Please, that would be so nice."

She returned with two glasses and set his down on the porch rail. "I sent one of the hands to fetch her for you."

"Rachel said it was a day's ride from Virginia City, but she didn't say that it would take all day long, although it is as beautiful a ride as I have ever seen. I didn't know that much green was in this state. I guess I thought that everything looked like the hills around Virginia City."

"That's why my husband and I settled here. We were headed for California and the gold country when we heard about this valley. When we saw it we stayed, and I never get tired of it."

"You say your husband. Is he here?"

"No, he was killed last year. Got pinned in the loading chute by a bull and was trampled. He and my son both were killed. Now it's just Rachel and me."

"You're her mother?" he asked.

"Yes, I am. If it wasn't for her I wouldn't know what would have happened to the ranch. She took on most of the responsibilities and has kept it going."

Rachel walked up the steps. "Mr. Mathews, I expected a letter from you."

"I thought I might as well see the other parts of Nevada if I am to practice law here. You weren't kidding when you said it was day's ride from Virginia City. I can see why you like this valley."

"Yeah, it is beautiful." She sat on the railing. "What did you find out?"

He took some papers out of a valise and gave them to her. "I checked about what you are saying, and it is most perplexing to say the least. No one I contacted has heard about a quarantine of any cattle in the area for any reason. I contacted the military in Sacramento and Washington D.C., and no one has any idea why you should be having this problem."

Rachel read the papers and gave them to Adele. She saw two men riding towards the house.

"I wonder what Sheriff Griffey and his deputy are doing out here?"

The sheriff and deputy stopped their horses at the porch.

"Evening, Sheriff. What brings you way out here?" Rachel asked.

"Howdy Rachel... Adele." He looked at Mathews but didn't say anything to him. "I'm here on official business. I need to speak to you and your mother."

Rachel looked at Mathews. "I have nothing to hide from anyone."

The sheriff dismounted and walked up the steps.

"Sometimes this job makes me do things I know ain't right, but I have to do what the law says for me to do." He took an envelope from his shirt pocket and gave it to Rachel. "I have to serve you notice that a lien has been placed on the ranch and that everything on it has to stay and cannot be removed."

"What?" Rachel grabbed the envelope and read the contents. "Who would put a lien on our ranch?"

"I don't know, but the notice came to me this morning," the sheriff said.

"Who the hell are Pittman, Carrier, and Wilson?" Rachel asked.

"I don't know, Rachel, but I know that that is a validated document and I have to serve you with it. There is some question as to whether Sean, and I guess you too Adele, gained the land for the ranch legally. A question has been raised about the tactics used in acquiring the land from the other ranchers."

"We bought and paid for all the land we own," Adele said. "We paid a good and fair price for all of it. How could this be happening?"

"I don't know, Ma. I don't know."

"Maybe I can be of some help," Mathews said. "Could I see the document?"

He took the paper from Rachel and read it.

"Sheriff, you say you have never heard of Pittman, Carrier, and Wilson?"

"Not around here." The sheriff shook his head.

"Hmm, this address is from Rock Springs, Wyoming. Wonder why someone from there would file a lien on a ranch out here?"

The sheriff mounted his horse. "I'm really sorry to bring you that. Sometimes I have to do my job even though I don't like it. I'm really sorry."

"I understand, Rodney," Adele said.

He started to say something else then tipped his hat to her and Rachel then rode away.

"What the hell are we gonna do now?" Rachel said. "We had planned to drive the cattle south to get whatever price we could, but now we can't even do that." She picked up a straight-backed chair and threw it across the porch. "What the hell is going on?"

"Rachel, calm down." Adele said. "It won't do any good to bust up the things we have."

"Calm down...calm down...I can't sell the cattle to the fort, then someone put a hold on our credit at the mercantile, and now someone is trying to get the ranch. So why should I calm down?"

"If you don't mind my saying something?" Mathews stood up.

"What?" Rachel bellowed at him.

He looked at her wondering if he should say anything.

"What would you like to say, Mr. Mathews?" Adele said.

He stood next to Adele.

"I will look into this matter if you would like."

"Yes, we would," Adele said.

"Rachel," Mathews said her name softly hoping she wouldn't throw something at him. "Rachel...."

"What?" She looked at him.

He held up the paper. "This lien goes into effect on tomorrow's date so you go ahead and get those cattle out of here. They are not quarantined that anyone knows about, and I am sure the sheriff won't miss a few head of cattle. I must be getting back to Virginia City."

"No," Adele said. "You will stay the night here. It's a fair ride to back Yerington let alone to Virginia City. We have plenty of room, so bring your things inside." She put her hand on Rachel's shoulder. "We have had some rough times, honey, and I know things look bad, but they will work out. Why don't you get ready for bed? You'll be up early for the drive tomorrow morning, and you need to be fresh."

"Get your things from the buggy, Mr. Mathews, and I'll take the horses to the barn," Rachel said. "Tell Ma for me that I'll be a while because I need some time to think."

Chapter Twenty-two

The old woman opened the door to the barn and walked to the last stall at the end of the aisle. "I'm gonna miss you, you old fart," she said to the old horse as she put the bit into its mouth. She threw a saddle on its back, and as usual she had to ram her knee into its side to make him exhale so she could get a good and tight grip with the cinch. He had been her horse for six years since she bought him from the government agent. Of all the horses she had he would be the best to make the long trip to Nevada. She led him out of the barn and tied him to the rail in front of the mission. She picked up the saddle bags from the porch and tied them to the back of the saddle then made sure the canteen had water. She turned when the screen door slammed shut.

"I've packed the bags and you have plenty of water for a while." She was trying her best not to cry.

Birdie stepped down from the wooden sidewalk. "I know you can't spare him and the food Clara. I told you that I can get on out of here on my own."

"No, I won't hear of it. I've ridden south a time or two, and it's no easy crossing for the men yet a woman alone. This here horse is used to traveling a ways and he won't be no bother for you. This way I feel better knowing that at least I gave you a good send off."

Birdie hugged the old woman. "I promise you I'll get him

back to you as soon as I can."

"Just let him have some good days with what days he has left." The old woman rubbed his forehead and leaned her head against his neck then wiped the tears from her face. "I'll miss you, Birdie. You take this and take care of yourself real good now."

Birdie didn't want to take the leather pouch because it had money in it—money the old woman saved for a long time and couldn't spare.

"I can't take your money."

"You'll need money and you know it. I'm just getting too old and where in tarnation am I going to spend it out here?"

Birdie took the pouch and gave her a hug. "I'll write to you and let you know how he is doing. I can't ever repay you for all that you've done for me."

"Child, you don't owe me anything. You did all the work just by living after the way we found you." She held Birdie's face in her hands. "Now you go on and get out of here before I change my mind and don't let him or you leave."

Birdie waved to Clara until she disappeared from view. It would take weeks of hard riding to get back home. The map Clara had pasted on the back wall of the school room was old, but it was good enough to plan her route from the mission near Klamath Falls back to Yerington. She thought about the last ten months at the mission. If it hadn't been for Clara and her son looking for their lost mule they wouldn't have found her. The mule stopped to graze alongside the river near where she had been left. They took her back to the mission and treated her wounds, not knowing if she would live or die. As she healed she became stronger and helped Clara and Joseph take care of the sick and injured soldiers and Indians. She thought about staying at the mission and not returning to the ranch because Rachel wouldn't understand what she had done, but Clara convinced her to go back.

Three days later she stopped at a trading post. A bell suspended on a leather string jingled when she opened the door.

"Can I help you?" a man asked as he walked into the mercantile from an adjoining room.

"I would like to buy some of that smoked beef you have hanging up there, some coffee, and a round of bread."

He stopped when he saw her. She knew it was because she was Indian that he didn't want to get the beef.

"You able to pay for it?" he asked.

She took the leather pouch out of her pocket and poured the money on the counter. "Is this enough?"

"Ah...yep, it is." He picked up a knife and waved it in the air.

She stepped back towards the door not knowing what he was planning to do.

"How much beef you need?"

"A long journey's worth," she said.

He wrapped the beef in a small piece of butcher paper then poured some coffee into a small bag. He put the coffee and a small loaf of bread into a flower sack with the beef.

"Are you riding alone?"

She didn't answer him.

"It ain't none of my business, I know, but the bounty hunters have been through here." He tied a string around the top of the sack. "You don't look like any of the Indians I seen around these parts, and from the way you carry yourself you ain't a reservation Indian. I just thought you'd like to know about them fellas being out there is all." He counted out thirty-six cents from the coins on the counter top and pushed the other coins back to Birdie. "They went northwest last time out."

"Thank you." She opened the door and looked up and down the street then mounted the old horse and rode off.

The rising sun helped burn the fog out of the valley, but the air was still damp and cold. Birdie sipped the coffee and held the cup in her hands to warm them. She tore off a piece of bread to eat with the beef. The old horse whinnied and raised his head to look over a bush. Birdie crouched under the horse to see what had spooked him. Two men on horseback followed by a wagon rode past. She waited until they were out sight then saddled the horse and rode away in the opposite direction.

She stopped that night next to a small lake, and although she was cold she didn't make a fire. She kept thinking about what the man at the mercantile had told her about the bounty hunters. She wrapped the blanket tightly around her body and tried to sleep. It was early the next morning when she saddled the horse and mounted it. She saw something flying at her from her left side then felt the rope as it tightened around her arms. She grabbed it and tried to take it off but was pulled backwards off the saddle onto the ground. Twisting around she came face to face with a large man holding a pistol. He yanked the rope again to keep her off balance when she tried to stand up.

"You can go on and keep trying to get away. I got you now, and you ain't going nowhere. No Indian ain't never got away from Indian Charlie yet."

He walked in a circle around her several times making sure not to get close enough for her to kick him. He spit at the ground then wiped his mouth with the sleeve of his shirt. Streaks of tobacco juice stained his scraggly, gray beard. He wore a dirty buckskin shirt with denim jeans and buckskin leggings. A large knife hung from his belt with a holster next to it for his pistol.

"Get up on your knees." When she didn't move he waved the pistol at her. "I'm gonna get a reward for you whether you're alive or dead, and the truth be known I don't care either way. One more dead squaw don't bother me none."

He tied her hands behind her back then pulled her up to her feet and pushed her to the horse.

"Where in the hell did you get that horse? It's got a government brand on it."

She didn't say anything. He helped her into the saddle then tied the reins of her horse to the pack of a mule.

They rode along a narrow trail through the trees turning northeast as the horses climbed up the mountain. Stopping on a ridge above a river they looked down on a campsite. A man was bent over a large stump sleeping. Indian Charlie pulled his rifle from the saddle scabbard and aimed it at the sleeping man. He fired three shots in rapid succession and laughed as the man jumped up then scrambled behind the stump for protection. The man peered over the stump and tried to grab his whiskey bottle, but it shattered when a bullet hit it. The man held up a stick with a white handkerchief and waved it in the air.

"I give up, I give up. Take what you want, just don't shoot me," he yelled. Indian Charlie and Birdie descended the hill.

"God damned it, Charlie, you could have kilt me. Even if you didn't shoot me." The man patted his body to make sure he wasn't hurt. "You scared the living daylights out of me. I cain't take any more of that and you know it."

"You been sucking on that bottle again, Willie? I told you if I caught you drinking again what I would do. We ain't got time for that. Hell you're supposed to be a ways further up river by now."

"The wagon broke an axle. Took me damned near all morning to get it back to working. With all I have to do by keeping them squaws a rounded up and fixing the god-damned axle I think I did a pretty bang up job of just getting here." Willie snorted. "I made sure they's all locked up good, real good. Looks like you got another one, huh?"

"Found her on the other side of the buttes. She's riding a government horse." He untied her horse from the mule pack. "She can't or won't tell me how she came by it."

"Looks like he's seen better days," Willie said. "Maybe he's one of them that they turn loose when it can't be of no use no more."

"I don't care where the horse came from. I just want my money for her." Charlie dismounted and spit at her. "Here, take her and tie her up to the wagon."

Willie led her horse to the wagon and helped her dismount.

"Sit down next to the wheel."

After she sat down he looped a leather strap around her

neck and tied it to one of the wheel spokes behind her head. He wrapped another strap around her ankles.

"Can I have my hands in front?" she asked him.

"What?"

"If I am to be bound like a hog for slaughter can I at least have my hands out in front of me?"

He looked over his shoulder at Charlie for a few seconds. "Yeah, I guess so. I guess you cain't get into too much trouble." He reached through the spokes and cut the rope with his knife. He grabbed her hands when she reached for the rope around her neck. "Don't try anything or I'll tie 'em back there again."

She held her hands out in front of him to let him tie her wrists together. When he left she leaned her head against the wheel and closed her eyes.

"Do not make trouble. They will give no mercy if you make trouble."

"Who are you?" Birdie tried to look into the wagon. "Where are they taking me?"

"We will speak when the time comes. We will meet then."

Indian Charlie banged on the door of the wagon with the butt of his rifle. "Shut up in there. I ain't in no mood to listen to you squaws yapping all night." He kicked Birdie's legs. "You shut up if you know what's good for you."

He sat next to the fire and drank some whiskey from a bottle. When the bottle was empty he threw it at Willie. "Get me a squaw."

"Oh piss damn hell, Charlie." Willie stomped to the wagon and opened the door. "You, you right there. Come with me."

He opened a bottle of whiskey and sat on a rock next to the fire to watch. The woman fought Charlie until his fist smashed into the side of her head and she fell backwards on the ground. She screamed in pain when Charlie forced himself inside her. He wrapped his hands around her throat and squeezed until she passed out. Birdie closed her eyes hoping that if she didn't watch she could keep her mind on other things. Charlie's grunting got louder and louder then he yelled and rolled off of her.

"She's yours," he said to Willie.

"About god damned time. I thought you'd never get through."

"It don't come too fast with a squaw. I prefer white women, but they'll do when I need it."

"I don't care if it's white or Indian, I get the same result."

Charlie took a drink of whiskey. "Your taste in women is why you ain't ever gonna be nothing but a mule skinner, Willie."

Willie wasn't paying any attention to Charlie.

Chapter Twenty-three

The first rays of sun over the mountain top woke Birdie. Willie didn't see her when she adjusted her body to get the pressure of the spoke away from her back and neck and tripped over her legs. He dropped the burlap sack and bucket he was carrying.

"Piss damn hell!" he yelled at her. "Watch where you put those things." He unlocked the door and threw the sack into the wagon then slammed the door shut. "Now I got to get more water."

After he put a new bucket full of water in the wagon he threw a piece of meat on her lap. She held up her hands for him to untie them.

"I ought not to even give you the meat for what you did to me." He stooped down beside her. "You won't do anything real cute now will you?"

"No."

"That's good because I ain't too happy with you." He slapped the side of the wagon with his fist. "I ain't too happy with any of you. You hear me?"

He untied the strap from both wrists then tied one arm to the wheel.

"Where's your partner?" Birdie asked.

Willie looked at the campsite. "He got to get to Camp Overland before we get there."

"Where is Camp Overland?"

"Over yonder mountain." He pointed to a peak north of where they were camped.

"What will happen at Camp Overland?"

Willie dipped some water out of the bucket with a tin cup and held it out for her. "You don't have any concern about that."

He stowed everything at the camp onto the pack mule then got a rifle from underneath the wagon seat, opened the door, and stepped back. "Okay, I need you to get things done, and I mean in a hurry. Two at a time like always."

Two women stepped out of the wagon. Neither said anything as they walked around until they had relieved themselves then stood at the door to get back into the wagon. When the last of the women were back inside the wagon he locked the door. He leaned the rifle against the wagon and took a pistol out of his waistband.

"I don't want no trouble from you," he said when he untied her hand then her legs.

She rubbed her wrists then leaned over to rub her legs. He jumped back away from her and pointed the pistol at her.

"I have to get some feeling in my legs before I can stand up." She stood up, holding onto the wagon for support. She looked at the women in the wagon then walked in a circle. After several minutes Willie yelled at her.

"You best get to getting busy 'cause we ain't got all day."

She walked as close to him as she dared and stopped. She could see his hand trembling. Was he nervous or was it because of all of the whiskey he drank the night before?

"Any closer and I'll shoot you dead right here." He cocked the hammer back.

If it was the whiskey she might have a chance to fight him, but she was still too far away to jump him to find out.

"Turn around so I can tie you up, then you get on your horse." He said.

He tied her hands to the saddle horn after she mounted the horse then tied the reins of her horse to the side of the wagon. Several hours later he took a bottle out of his saddle bag and drank a large gulp.

"You don't look like any Indian I ever seen around here before. You have good speech, too. Where you from?" He asked her.

"I am from the Mason Valley ranch in the state of Nevada. On the ranch we raise beef and alfalfa."

"Uh huh, and I am the president of these here United States. Ain't no goddamned Indians got beef or alfalfa. You Indians steal from hard working folks. You are in pretty big trouble for having that there government horse, too. Where did you steal him from?" He took another gulp of whiskey. "I bet some commander of the fort that you stole him from is right hopping mad at some soldier for letting a Indian woman get away with one of his horses."

"I didn't steal him. He was given to me by the care taker of the mission at Fort Klamath."

"You mean that you duped some soldier into thinking you was his woman then took off with it?"

"I've been to the Klamath nation," A voice from the wagon said.

Birdie looked into the wagon to see who was talking to her.

"I was a young girl. My father was there to make peace with the Klamath and the Modoc. We were there for three moons until the winter."

"Who are you?" Birdie asked.

"I am Amora of the Bitter Root."

"I don't know where that is," Birdie said.

"I do not know of the land where you tell of. What is your name?"

"Birdie."

"Why are you here?" Amora asked.

"I was going back home to the Mason Valley when Indian Charley captured me. He said I was worth money."

"You go now with us to Bitter Root Val...."

"Shut up." The whiskey bottled shattered when Willie

threw it at the wagon. "I don't want to hear any more of that yapping."

"We talk later," Amora said.

Willie drank from another bottle. "I get tired of his almighty lord and master Indian Charley getting all the easy work and money whilst I have to sit here with you dirty stinking squaws."

Chapter Twenty-four

Willie stopped the wagon on the top of a hill and pointed down at a narrow valley. "That is where I get rid of the likes of you." He drank the last of the whiskey and threw the bottle on the ground then drove the wagon into a small encampment of cavalry troops. One large tent had a guard posted in front of it. Three other large tents were off to the left and facing the smaller two rows of tents aligned to face each other. Willie drove the wagon behind the smaller tents and stopped the wagon in front of a fenced area.

Indian Charlie walked out of a tent. "You been drinking again."

"Well if you don't like it then you can get your ass out here and bring them in your own self."

"We don't need any animosity gentlemen," a soldier said. "Sergeant, put these women into the compound."

"Yes sir, Captain." The sergeant waved at Willie to follow him. When the wagon lurched forward the captain shouted at Willie to stop.

"What is she doing on that horse?" He pointed at Birdie.

"I dunno, Captain," Indian Charlie said. "I captured her with it. She ain't much for talking so I don't rightly know how she got it."

The captain walked around the horse then said to Birdie. "Can you understand what I am saying?"

Birdie looked at him for a few seconds before answering. "Clearly."

"Do you have a name?"

"Birdie Perez."

"Where did you come by that horse?"

"This horse was given to me by the caretaker of the mission at Fort Klamath for my journey back home."

"You don't look or speak like a northern Indian. Where are you from?"

"I live in the Mason Valley on a ranch outside of Yerington in the state of Nevada."

"You speak very well."

"I have been to school in the Mason Valley."

The captain took a knife from his belt and started to cut the rope from around her wrists.

"Just a god damned minute, Captain Borders," Indian Charlie said. "You can't do that."

"I can do anything I want. I am the commander here, and she isn't to be treated like the others." He cut the rope. "Even you, Charlie, should be able to see that she isn't from around here. And with speech like that it is very apparent she isn't a reservation Indian."

"No matter what she is or isn't she's still worth something." Charlie grabbed the reins of her horse. "I brung her in, and I intend to get my money for her."

The captain spun around to face him. "If I say you get something then you will get something. I will find out of she is telling the truth, and if she is you will get nothing."

"Taint fair," Charlie said.

"Sergeant, get that wagon into the compound. This one will stay with me a while."

The sergeant saluted and waved for Willie to follow him.

"Follow me," the captain said to Birdie as he walked into the large tent. Indian Charlie stepped in front of her when she tried to follow the captain.

"If 'fin you don't move I'll shoot," the guard standing in front of the tent said to Charlie as he lowered his rifle. Charlie spit tobacco juice at Birdie's feet as she walked past him.

The captain was sitting behind a small desk. He pointed at a chair. "Please sit down."

"I prefer to stand."

"I am not going to hurt you, Miss Perez. I need to get some information so we can get you home."

"Why do you care if I get home?"

"Well, for one thing it is very clear to me that you aren't from around here by your speech, and you surely don't carry yourself like a reservation Indian either." He walked around the desk and stood next to a map of the United States hanging on the wall of the tent. He waved his hand at her. "Come here."

She didn't move.

"I came out of West Point in time for the war between the states. I was young and in love with the romance of war and battle. After five years of watching men on both sides get butchered for a cause, justifiable or not, I am no longer in love with the idea of war." He sat back down at the desk. "I came out west thinking I could find a new way of life. Unfortunately, I have gotten myself back into the thick of senseless killing and lawlessness. I've seen what happens to Indians as they try to retain their way of life only to be pushed off their land for gold or cattle. I can't stop the westward migration of settlers, but I try to help the Indians as much as I can. I can only guess what it must be like to be imprisoned on a reservation. I am at this camp because me and my commander at the fort don't agree on how to treat those women out there in the compound. Men like Indian Charlie out there work for the government looking for runaways and get money for capture and return to the reservation. They capture them and bring them back to camps like this. God only knows how many never make it back." He started pacing back and forth in front of the desk. "We escort them back to the reservation where there's not enough food or water or warm clothes in the winter. No wonder they try to escape. I made myself a vow that as long as I am out here I will make damned sure that they will be fed good and given decent clothing and treated like human beings rather than dogs. I guess that I am in some ways trying to make up for the mistakes of the United States government." He sat at the desk and dipped a pen in an ink bottle. "I can send a wire to someone who can vouch for you. If I get a favorable reply you can be on your way. I'll give you a letter of freedom to take with you should there be a need."

Birdie didn't know if she should believe him. He was not a man of the large stature one would have thought a cavalry captain should be, but his mannerisms and speech certainly got one's attention. It was easy to see why his commander put him in charge of this camp. She looked at the map thinking about what the captain had said. Even if he did what he said who could she tell him to contact?

"Send the wire to Rachel O...." She stopped. Would Rachel answer the wire? If he received no reply what would she do then? "The sheriff knows of me. The sheriff of Yerington, Nevada."

"I'll send the wire to the sheriff of Yerington, Nevada." He wrote the name on a piece of paper. "I would like to offer you a tent out there, but none is available at this moment. Even if I did it would not be too safe for you as some of the men under my command do not share my views. For your own safety I must ask that you join the other women in the compound at the back of the camp."

Birdie shook her head. "I understand, captain."

"Private Garson."

The guard at the door of the tent stepped inside and saluted the captain. "Yes sir?"

"Please escort Miss Perez to the compound."

"Sir, might I say something?"

"Yes private, what is it?"

The soldier looked at the captain, then at Birdie. "Sir, I was just thinking that she don't...uh...look...uh...I mean...she don't seem like a reservation Indian, and I don't think that she should be in the compound with the others...sir."

"Private, I quite understand what you're saying, but I think that with some of the men we have stationed out in the barracks tents at the moment it would be most prudent if we put her in the compound to keep them away from her."

The private thought about what the captain said. "I guess you would be right about that, sir. I'll be escorting her to the compound now."

"Thank you, private."

The private saluted the captain then stepped away from the door to let Birdie pass. "Ma'am."

Birdie followed the private along a path to the compound. Some of the men stopped working when they passed, but no one said anything. Indian Charlie sat on a barrel in front of the last tent. He stood up in front of the private to block the path.

"Get out of the way, Charlie," the private said.

"You and your Indian loving captain ain't gonna keep me from getting my money for her, private."

"I don't want no trouble, Charlie. I just gotta take her to the compound. Let us by."

Charlie pulled his knife out of the scabbard. "If you think you can best me then go ahead. After I cut your guts out I'll take care of her."

"Knock it off, Charlie," another soldier said to Charlie as he walked up to them. "She ain't going nowhere, just like the rest of them."

Charlie grabbed Birdie's wrist and waved the knife in front of her. "It don't matter if you're walking, crawling, or not moving. You're mine and I'm going to get my money."

Birdie jerked her arm away from him and stepped closer to the private.

"I'll see that you get what's coming to you," the soldier said. "You know it's gonna be a day or two till they are to be taken out of here. There's a card game in Milo's tent, and we can get in on it."

Charlie sat back down on the barrel to let them pass. He spit tobacco juice at her feet. "If anything happens I'm gonna make sure that that squaw bitch gets it my own self."

Chapter Twenty-five

The guard on duty opened a small door to the left of the main gate into the compound. The walls of the compound were made up of tall wooden stakes lashed together with jute cord with openings to see outside every six feet. The back wall was a natural rock wall that towered over the camp. A large tree provided shade in the middle area with four others at the base of the rock wall. The women were gathered under the trees at the wall and watched as Birdie walked in. She walked along the edge of the fence, but none came forward to speak to her.

"No escape from here."

Birdie recognized the voice.

"If you get over they shoot like dog."

"You're from the wagon," Birdie said to the woman.

"You go with us to Bitterroot. Always they take us to Bitterroot."

"I will go home to Yerington."

"You go with us."

Birdie wondered why the woman was so sure she would go to a place called Bitterroot. She started to ask the woman why she would be going with them when a wagon with three soldiers on it drove through the gates and stopped near the middle of the compound. One soldier poured water from a barrel in the wagon into a barrel on the ground while another soldier dropped three sacks on the ground. None of the women moved until the wagon had left and the gates were shut. Several women surrounded the sacks, but no one touched them until Amora picked one up. She took a loaf of bread out of the sack and talked to another woman in a language Birdie had never heard then grabbed a slab of dried meat out of the sack the woman held.

"Come." Amora motioned for Birdie to follow her to the back of the compound. She offered half the bread and meat to Birdie when they sat down under a tree.

"How long do they keep you here?" Birdie asked.

"Sometimes many days."

"Are all of them from your land?"

"No." Amora bit into the dried beef. "They are looking for family so they leave the white man's reservation. Men not go to same reservation." Amora pointed at a young woman. "She lost husband in fight with cavalry two moons ago. She looks for mother's sister. She is with baby soon and need to find family to live with. They all go to the Bitterroot."

"Are you looking for family too?" Birdie asked

"No."

"Why don't you stay in your reservation where it is safe?"

Amora put down the food and stood up. She held her hands and arms high in the air. "I am the daughter of Standing Wolf, leader of our tribe of Nez Perce. He was killed in battle two winters ago. I was to be the wife to son of Red Moon, but he was killed in battle with my father. I am the daughter of a chief so I must find the women and lead them to freedom. I take them to grandmother's land of Canada. I come back to take them many times." She sat back down. "You go with us to Bitterroot."

Birdie nibbled at the bread and meat. She thought about what Amora had said and didn't want to go anywhere but back to Yerington and the ranch. She wondered if the sheriff in Yerington would remember her and answer the wire. She wondered if Rachel thought about her anymore. She wondered if Rachel would love her if she knew what she had done.

Amora walked around the compound to check on the rest of the women. It was easy to see the women held Amora in high regard. She made sure the oldest women were closest to the fire pit and everyone had enough to eat. As the sun gave way to darkness she finally sat down at the base of the tree and went to sleep. Birdie tried to sleep but couldn't stop thinking about Rachel and the ranch. It was late in the night when she finally dozed off.

The sound of gunshots woke everyone. They all ran to the fence to see what was happening. A rider galloped into the camp with two wagons following him. The captain came out of his tent pulling up his suspenders and yelling at the man to stop the shooting.

"Top o' the morning to ya, captain." The man spun his horse around in a circle a couple of times as he spoke. "Tis I, Yancey Gilbraithe, at your service and I got quite a haul for ya."

The captain looked into the wagons. "Corporal, get the doctor and have him meet me in the compound."

"Yes, sir."

"Mr. Gilbraithe, I told you that I wouldn't stand for this kind of treatment of them any more."

"Well captain, you aren't the one rounding them up and bringing them back, are ya?"

"Sergeant, take these wagons to the compound—now."

Gilbraithe charged into the compound when the sentry opened the gates. He fired his pistol in the air, scattering the women. He chased two of them and kicked them to the ground with his boot. When he turned the horse to go back out of the gate Birdie grabbed a bucket that was hanging on the wall. She jumped onto a rock and swung it at him as he rode by. The bucket hit him in the chest, knocking him off the horse backward. He pulled his pistol from his belt.

The captain wrestled it from him. "I'll have no shooting in this compound."

"That bitch deserves it," Gilbraithe shouted at him.

"One more word and I'll do the shooting and it won't be her." The captain stood between Birdie and Gilbraithe. "Do you hear me?"

Walking out of the compound he stopped and pointed at her. "No bitch hits me and gets away with it."

The doctor ran into the compound. "What do you need, captain?"

"Gilbraithe," the captain said and pointed at the wagons.

The doctor looked inside the wagons. "Okay, let's get them out of there. Private Crosley, go back to the infirmary and bring me the field box. You men help get them out of there."

Birdie watched as Amora and the soldiers helped get the women out of the wagons. The guard yelled that another wagon was coming into the compound. The driver yelled at the women to get out of the way, then pulled the horses to a stop.

"What the hell do you think you're doing?" the doctor said.

"Getting here that's what. I got twenty dollars bet on these nags." The driver stood up and looked around the compound. "Gilbraithe's not here yet, is he?"

"I'll take that twenty dollars now, Shorty." Gilbraithe stood next to the gate. "What took you so long? You passed me two days ago."

Shorty held up a braid of hair in his hand. "Had a little squaw problem, but she won't be bothering anyone now. Chased that bitch clean up the mountain, I did. I thought that if fin I brung this then it should be worth something."

"Give me that," the captain said.

"It's mine," Shorty snorted.

"Give it to me or you'll not get any money for any of them."

"You can't do that."

"I can do anything I want as the commander of this camp."

Shorty scratched the beard under his chin and spit on the ground. "What the hell, I ain't got no use for it and neither does that squaw bitch." He threw it at the captain's feet.

"I got some whiskey, Shorty," Gilbraithe said as he walked

away from the gate. "Let the Indian lover have that and his women."

"Well doc I'd love to stay and help but I have a bet to settle."

"Son of a bitch, just once I wish I could put regulations behind me." The doctor said when Shorty left. "You, soldier, give me a hand here."

Before the soldier could move Amora climbed onto the wagon. The doctor looked at her for a moment then gave her a bandage. Birdie grabbed the field box and stepped onto the wagon to help. After the last woman had been cared for they all sat down next to the fence.

"How do you know so much about medicine?" the doctor asked Birdie.

"I learned at Fort Klamath. I was found...I stayed with a missionary woman and her son last winter and helped them with the soldiers and Indians."

"They taught you well." He smiled at her then said to Amora, "You are a very good student, too."

The doctor grabbed the field box and his black case. "I will be back later tonight to check on them. Don't hesitate to have the guards get me if anyone needs help."

Birdie followed Amora as she walked around the compound talking to each woman. She checked bandages and listened as they talked to Amora in their native tongues and was amazed that Amora could talk to each of them. The women seemed to accept their fate and were a lot more at ease with Amora. When everyone had been tended to they sat down.

"How do you know so many tongues?" Birdie asked her.

"I learned from my uncle. He was a shaman. As a little girl I would follow him and ask about his medicine and healing power. He would take me to far away lodges to take care of the sick and dying. He was wise and known in other lands as a great shaman. He said it was an honor to be a shaman. He said that one doesn't choose to be a healer but it chooses who should be. I am the oldest of my father's daughters, and

I was chosen. He talked to others in their tongue when we visited and he taught me."

"Why don't you stay in the land of Canada?"

"I am a chief's daughter and a shaman. I have to keep using my power to get them to Canada to safety. Our land was taken by the white man for gold and cattle. They shoot our buffalo and make us live on reservation. I go look for my people and any others to take them to safety in the land of my elders."

"I have heard of Canada," Birdie said, remembering Big Jake.

"It is many days from here. We will cross the white man's border and we will be free."

"How do you plan to get out of here?"

"I will go back to the Bitterroot reservation with the soldiers and wait for my uncle. You will go with us. Then we will go to Canada."

"I can't. I must get back to the ranch. I want to go home."

"You will see that you must go with us to Canada. You will go with us." Amora leaned against the fence and pulled a blanket over her arms. "You will see."

Chapter Twenty-six

The rays of the morning sun were creeping over the walls of the compound when the gates opened to let in the wagon with the food and water. The soldiers filled the barrel with water, dropped the sacks, and left. Birdie followed Amora and helped her distribute the food to the women who were brought in by Gilbraithe. She kept looking at the gate, hoping the captain would come in and tell her that she could go home. A woman called to Amora that she was needed at the back of the compound. Squatting, moaning, and holding on to a tree was the young pregnant woman. It was obvious she was in trouble with the birth. Amora talked to the woman trying to help her.

"Something's wrong," Amora said to Birdie. "Go get doctor."

Birdie ran to the guard shack and pounded on the door next to the gate. A soldier slid the cover of the window back to look at her.

"Get the doctor."

"What for?" the soldier asked.

"We need the doctor. She's having trouble with the birth."

"Soon as I finish my grub." He slammed the window shut.

She looked around the compound then picked up a log from the wood pile and threw it against the gate until the soldier opened the window again.

"Knock it off," he yelled.

"We need the doctor."

He opened the door and pointed a rifle at her. "If you don't shut up that noise I'm gonna shoot. I said when I'm finished with my grub."

He ducked to get out of the way when she threw the log at him and he fired a bullet into the ground. He raised the rifle to shoot her but dropped it when she threw dirt into his eyes. He stumbled backwards out of the compound and she started to run to find the doctor, but another soldier grabbed her.

"Hold her right there," the guard yelled. "I'm gonna take some hide for that." He cuffed her with the back of his hand then grabbed her hair and pulled her head back. "I'm gonna make you sorry that you did that."

"Corporal, if you hit that woman again I'll see you in the stockade for a long while," the captain yelled at him.

"Well goddamn it, she deserves it. Look at what she did to me."

"It's just a scratch." The captain stood between them. "Now what is going on?"

"She started a ruckus by hitting the door with that log there. I told her to quiet down, but she kept on, and when I opened the door to quiet her down she threw the log at me then threw dirt in my eyes."

"Is that true?" the captain asked Birdie.

"Yes, but we need the doctor."

"What's the matter?"

Birdie pointed into the compound. "One of the women is birthing and needs help from the doctor."

"You stay here." The captain pointed at the guard. "You soldier, you go get the doctor and get him here now." He followed Birdie to where the woman was lying on the ground.

The doctor pushed his way through the women. "What's going on?"

"This woman needs your attention. She is birthing and needs some help."

The doctor knelt down next to the woman. "She's dead,

captain."

"So is he." Amora was holding the baby.

"There is nothing I can do here now captain."

"Jesus have mercy on their souls," the captain said in a low voice then bellowed at a soldier. "Sergeant!"

"Yes sir?"

"Sergeant, round up a couple of men and bury them. Bury them like you would your own."

"I am truly sorry," the captain said then left.

"It's a pity...such a pity and I can't do a thing about it," the doctor said. "I'll be back in a while to see to the women brought in yesterday."

The soldiers put the woman on a stretcher and waited for Amora to lay the baby next to her. She looked at Birdie with tears in her eyes. "I told her I would take her to her family."

Birdie took the baby from Amora and put it on the stretcher. She sat next to Amora and held her as she cried. The afternoon shade had disappeared when the doctor entered the compound.

"I will leave my grandmother's land of Canada no more." She looked around the compound at the women. "I must take care of the women."

Amora and Birdie followed the doctor. Neither one spoke unless they were asked a question. They were at the far end of the compound when the gate opened and a soldier walked in.

"I need Birdie Perez and the woman called Amora." He put his hands on his hips. "I ain't got all day."

"I'm Birdie Perez." She walked up to the soldier.

"I am Amora."

"Well, then follow me. The captain wants to see you."

Private Garson smiled when he saw Birdie walking up the path to the tent. He saluted her and pulled back the flap on the tent to let them in. Captain Borders put the papers he was reading down on the desk.

"Miss Perez, I am glad to see you again." He held his hand out to Amora. "I haven't met you personally, but I have heard many good things about you from the company doctor." When she didn't shake his hand he motioned for them to sit down in the chairs in front of the desk. "Please sit down."

He didn't push the issue when neither one of them sat down. "I have been at this post for only eight months, but I have heard about your exploits from the states to Canada, Miss Amora. You are a very brave woman to do what you do in spite of all the difficulties afforded you. Although I do agree with you and your thoughts on the treatment of the Indians here, I must tell you that I have received word from my commander at the fort that you are to be taken to the fort for trial. I don't need to tell you what will happen to you if you are taken there. I am going to offer you safe passage back to the reservation if you promise to stay there and not go on any more expeditions to get your people. If you leave the reservation there will be a heavy bounty on your head and it will bring the worst of the trackers to find you. I don't have to tell you that they don't have a sense of decency and they won't care if you come back alive." He stopped talking to let her think about what he had said. "I will not send you to the fort if you promise me you will stay on the reservation and not leave for any reason. If you don't promise me that then I have no recourse but to send you to the fort."

Amora walked around the tent thinking about what the captain had said. She raised the flap to look at the mountains. "My people have walked the land of the Bitterroot from time past until the white man took it away from us. We cannot live on reservation because we cannot feed ourselves. You take our bow and arrows from us so we cannot hunt the buffalo. You tell us we will be fed but not enough food is given to eat. When we are sick we must wait too long for white doctor because the medicine man has been taken away. I only do what is needed for my people."

"I understand and I know what you are saying, but you must understand that it takes time for things to get better. Not all white men are like that. I must ask you, in fact I implore you, do not leave the reservation again as I am worried what would happen to you of you are caught again."

"I will go back to the reservation to care for my people. I will think about your words." Amora looked into the eyes of the captain with a look of defiance. "If my people cannot live then I will do what is needed to care for them."

"I only wish I had men with your resolve in my command." He knew that the future would be difficult for her and hoped she would make it out alive. "Miss Perez, I am still waiting to hear from the sheriff. We have had some skirmishes along the Idaho Nevada border and the wires have been cut. I hope to get an answer soon. Is there anything I can do to ease your stay here?"

"No," Birdie said.

"No," Amora said.

Chapter Twenty-seven

Three days later the guard on the tower called Birdie's name and told her to stand at the gate. Another guard opened the gate to let the captain enter.

"I received an answer from Yerington. The sheriff knows of you and said to send you home."

Birdie couldn't believe what he had said. "What?"

"You can go home, Miss Perez. I will have the men get your horse and possessions together for you. You can leave now if you want."

"No, I will leave in the morning."

"I will have the men get the extra tent ready for you to stay in tonight."

She looked back at the compound. "No, I will stay here with them."

"Are you sure?" he asked. "You are a free woman and you don't have to stay with them."

"Yes, I am sure."

"If I had just a few men with the resolve of you two women I would be happy." He smiled at her. "I'll see you in the morning."

Amora put her arm around Birdie's shoulder when she told her what the captain had said. "It is good that you go home."

Birdie didn't say anything.

"You see family now."

"If they will have me."

Amora was puzzled at the response but decided not to pursue it.

The next morning Birdie looked back at Amora as the guard closed the gate. She followed the soldier to the captain's tent. Private Garson smiled and tipped his hat at her.

"Well, Miss Perez, I hope you have a good journey," the captain said. "I trust you will be careful and watch out for those damned bounty hunters. I know you want to go home, but I'm not sure this is the right thing for you to do alone."

"I will be very careful and stay off the main roads captain."

"Watch out for Indian Charlie and Gilbraithe. They plan to leave tomorrow and I know how they think. You will be heavy on their minds." He opened a drawer and offered her a leather pouch. "Here is your money and your belongings are on your horse."

"Thank you, Captain Bowers." She took the money and walked out of the tent.

"I've instructed Private Garson to escort you to the end of the valley. I want to make sure that Indian Charley and Gilbraithe don't do anything funny." He saluted her. "I bid you goodbye and a lot of luck, Miss Perez."

She saluted back. "You are a good man, captain, and I hope you live long enough to see your dreams and thoughts come true."

"Be back in a little while, sir," Private Garson said to the captain as they rode away.

Birdie looked back at the compound as she rode away from the camp.

"Excuse me for talking ma'am, but isn't it a bit scary for you to be riding alone? I mean, no offense, ma'am, but they caught you once before and well I'd be right concerned about those two being out here."

"I guess it is to be worried about so I'll have to be more careful than usual."

"I'm sorry to see you leave, ma'am. I think you are a very

nice looking Indian woman." His face turned red at the statement. "No...I mean that I think that you are a very nice woman and pleasing to look at." He took is hat off and wiped his brow with the shirt sleeve. "I don't mean no offense, ma'am."

"No offense taken, private." Birdie smiled at him.

"I...I wish I could find a woman like you, but I get no chance to meet the women they bring to the compound. I ain't got no one else in this life and I see some of them women back there and they sure look good."

"Maybe if you talked to the captain about it he would understand and let you meet some of them."

"I would like that. Maybe I could ask...what the hell?" The corporal pulled his pistol out of the holster when gunshots rang out.

Birdie also heard the shots and turned to see a band of warriors attacking the camp. She heard more gun shots and saw riders coming towards her and the private. He turned his horse around to get back to the camp. She knew she couldn't get out of the way of the approaching riders so she braced herself for whatever would happen, but they rode past her. The old cavalry horse's instincts took over to join in the battle, and he started chasing them. It was all she could do to get control of him, then another band of riders rushed past them and he bolted after them. She finally turned him around to get out of the valley then she heard the screams of the women in the compound.

Indian Charlie and Willie were standing on opposite sides of the compound shooting at the women. She looked at the opening of the valley and freedom then looked at the women in the compound. She pulled the gun from her belt and kicked the horse in the sides. As the old horse raced towards the fence she started shooting at Willie. He didn't notice her until a bullet ricocheted off the post and grazed his forehead. He grabbed his head and looked up to see her riding towards him. He stood up to aim his rifle at her, but it was too late. The horse hit him, slamming his body into the fence. She turned the horse around to charge at him again, but she could see that Willie had a broken neck.

The women in the compound were running in all directions away from Indian Charlie's shots. She took the rope from the saddle and tied it to the top of a fence post then wrapped the other end around the saddle horn. When she kicked the old horse in the sides he lunged forward, but the fence wouldn't budge.

"Son of a bitch," she yelled and kicked the horse again. This time he lunged with so much force she almost fell off. She heard a loud snap and felt the fence give a little. "Once more, old man." He seemed to understand what she wanted and lunged harder. The post snapped, bringing the fence down with it. She rode around the compound yelling at the women to get out.

"Come with me this way," she yelled to Amora as she rode around the compound. A bullet ripped through her arm and another flew by her head. She looked up to see Indian Charlie aiming his rifle at her again. She rode toward him, firing her pistol. He jumped out of the way then spun around to shoot the rifle but missed her. She turned the horse and pulled the trigger on the pistol, but it was empty. She chased after him as he started running away from the compound then kicked him to the ground with her boot. She jerked the reins hard to the left to make the horse reel around, knocking him back down to the ground again when he tried to stand up. As he went down he grabbed at her foot. She took her rifle out of the scabbard and swung it at his head. He rolled away from the horse and stumbled over the body of a dead soldier. Grabbing the soldier's pistol, he turned around to shoot her, but the last thing he saw was the barrel of a rifle pointed at his face.

After the rifle had been emptied and the fighting was over, Birdie kept squeezing the trigger as she stood over the body of Indian Charlie until a warrior placed his hand on the barrel. It was only then that she noticed how quiet it was. She looked at the warrior then at the camp. Smoke from the flames was all that was left of the tents. The ground was littered with bodies of the dead soldiers. The women of the compound were standing behind the braves. She slowly walked around the camp looking at the destruction. She walked past the last tent and heard someone call her name.

"Miss Perez, please help me." Captain Borders was lying in the ruins of the tent.

She saw blood oozing from between his fingers as he grasped at the wound in his belly. "I'm not sure how I can help you, captain."

"I'm gut shot. Please don't leave me like this...I beg of you, please don't leave me like this." He grabbed her arm. "Please."

She looked around the compound at the bodies of the dead soldiers until she found a pistol with bullets in it. A warrior stepped in front of her to take the gun.

Birdie looked at Amora. "He doesn't deserve to be left like that."

The warrior stepped aside when Amora spoke to him. Birdie stood next to the captain, cocked the pistol, and aimed it at his head. Slowly she lowered the pistol and put it in his hand. "Goodbye, captain."

"Thank you, Miss Perez. May god bless you."

She didn't look back when she heard the shot. She mounted the horse when Amora spoke.

"You go with us now."

"I can't." Birdie started riding away. "I have to go home."

"No. When soldiers come back they will look for us. You are Indian just as we are and cannot change that. No one will help you."

Birdie stopped the horse. Amora was right. She was Indian, and no matter what she did she couldn't change it. She looked around the camp to see the women stripping clothing from the dead and the men taking guns and ammunition. Birdie watched them walk north out of the valley after Amora called them together. She understood what Amora was saying. She knew what the white man thought of her kind. She had been a slave to them and had seen Indian women killed as if they were curs on the streets. She had to fight for her own life because of white men. If she went north with them she would never see Rachel again. She looked to the south end of the valley. If she went back to the ranch would Rachel remember her? Would Rachel understand and want her back knowing what she had done?

Chapter Twenty-eight

Rachel stopped the wagon alongside the alfalfa field to watch Stony, one of the hands, mow the field. Maybe they could get one more cutting before winter set in for good. The nights had already started to cool down, and the sun peeked over the mountains later each morning. The summer season had been long and easy with the alfalfa and grasses knee high to the cattle. The cattle were fat and ready to sell. She would have to take them south again to get away from the quarantine. Mr. Mathews had said that until the sheriff, who didn't seem to care, told her not to sell the cattle or arrested her for violation of the order she could sell them. Going south would take longer, but if they left before the other ranchers she could get a good price for them. She waved at Stony then continued on to Yerington.

No one knew who ordered the quarantine of the ranch or why. The lien was still against the ranch, but Mathews said no one had come forward to claim on it. He sent detectives to Denver then Washington D.C. but still no answers. She had milk, fresh eggs, and canned fruit in the back of the wagon for the mercantile. On her way home she planned to stop at Job Ferguson's ranch to get their bull. Job wanted five of the newborns if the bull produced like he did this year.

She missed her father and his simple way of talking and working. She had learned a lot about ranch work from him but knew that she still didn't know half the things he did. She thought about her mother and how she continued to maintain the house and help out in the stockyards when an extra hand was needed. She missed Jacob and his laugh. Everyone loved it when he was around. It sure would be nice if they could see the ranch and how she was keeping it going in spite of everything.

She tried to keep her mind on her father and Jacob because she didn't want to start thinking about Birdie. Whenever she was alone she couldn't keep her mind from thinking about her. She tried not to think of her, but sometimes, most of the time, her heart overruled her mind. If she could keep busy with the chores she could keep her mind occupied thinking about the task at hand. But at times like these when she had to go to Yerington by herself or when she and her mother would sit out on the front porch in the evening she couldn't stop the memories. She wondered why no one at the fort knew where Birdie and her brothers went. Surely if they were the ones to take them they would know if they were on the reservation. No one could answer her questions, and she hadn't received an answer from the letter she wrote to the Bureau of Indian Affairs. It was strange that Birdie hadn't tried to contact her.

She backed the wagon up to the loading dock in back of the mercantile and rang the bell for Seth to open the door. After the delivery had been made she went to the bank to deposit the money.

"How's everything going, Rachel?" the clerk asked when she pushed the money under the window.

"Fine."

"I hear the Weller boys have a good crop of feed this year and they will be taking their cattle on up north in a few days."

"That's good. We got a good cutting the last few days, and I'm hoping to get another one before the snow flies. Maybe it won't be as tall as the others but still it helps."

"Yeah, this had been a good year for everyone." He finished writing on a piece of paper and shoved it under the window.

"Thanks," Rachel said and walked out the door.

"Good afternoon, Rachel." Major Wilson was standing next to the wagon with his foot propped on the hub of the wheel. "Sergeant Crowley and I are about to dine at Miss Nell's cafeteria. Would you like to join us?"

She deliberately used the hub as a step to get onto the wagon to make him take his foot off of it. "No."

"Oh come on, Rachel, it wouldn't hurt. It's just a meal and some company."

"I have things to do this afternoon and don't want to be too late getting back to the ranch." She picked up the reins.

He put his hand on her arm and spoke in a low voice when she looked at him. "Rachel, you need to think about what is going to happen to you and your ranch. That place is too big for a woman to handle alone. You need more that a few hired hands to keep it viable."

"I'm doing just fine."

He squeezed her arm with his hand. "You need a man around to help."

"I don't need any man around to run my ranch." She jerked her arm away.

"I have tried several times these last few months to get to know you a little better. If you would ease up on your way of thinking you would see that I could be a lot of help to you. You have to be prepared for any problems that a ranch like that can have."

"Such as?"

"Well, for one thing, you aren't getting any younger, and I have noticed that there aren't a lot of men around the valley knocking at your door. If you want that ranch to survive you need a husband. A man would know how to run a spread that big and could give you sons to help. That would be the best thing for the ranch."

"Go to hell, major." She slapped the reins on the horses.

"It's not right that a ranch like that is in the hands of a woman. She's cocky now, but we will see what is to come.

Before it's over she will come begging to me for help," he said as he watched her drive away. "I have less than four years to go until I can retire from the cavalry, and I do not plan to spend my retirement living on a soldier's pay."

Rachel ate dinner at the Ferguson's ranch house, tied the bull to the back of the wagon, and left for home. The road from Ferguson's ranch to hers crossed the road that followed the creek to the springs. It had been almost a year since she had been this close to them. If she didn't follow that road it would be another hour until she was back at the ranch, and she wasn't in the mood to deal with an ornery bull. She stopped at the top of the rise between the hot and cold ponds and thought about the many times she and Birdie had been there. Closing her eyes, she could see Birdie standing next to the pond and teasing her. It didn't take much before she would chase after her then they would make love. All the times they had made love here was never like the last time at the line shack—the vows they said to each other, then the way Birdie caressed her kissed her and made love to her then demanded the same intensity in return. It was if they were one. It was as if they would never see each other again.

"Why in the hell didn't you tell me, Birdie?" Rachel said out loud, hoping for an answer while knowing no answer would come.

She led the bull into the pen and shut the gate, locking it as she walked out of the pen. She led the horse into the barn after unhitching it from the buggy.

Arturo ran into the barn and grabbed the reins from her hand. "Rachel, you must go inside quickly."

"What's wrong Arturo?"

"It's you're mother...she's...."

Rachel ran to the house, not waiting for his answer. She saw the doctor's black coat on the back of a chair and ran up the stairs. The doctor was sitting on the edge of her mother's bed and stood up as she ran into the room. She walked around the bed, looking at her mother.

"What's going on, doc?"

"I think she's had a stroke."

She sat on the bed and picked up her mother's hand. "Is she gonna be all right?"

"I don't know, Rachel. Sometimes it takes a while before we really know anything. It could be a day or two before we can tell anything for sure."

"Ma, it's me. You're gonna be all right, you hear me? You gotta be all right."

The doctor watched Rachel for awhile then spoke. "Rachel, I think you need to prepare yourself for...," he looked at the floor to keep from looking at her. "Her breathing is shallow and her heart is very weak."

"What are you saying, doc?"

"If she lives she will most likely be bedridden."

She listened to him talking and watched her mother struggle to breathe. She covered her face with her hands, hoping that when she removed them everything would be all right.

"I don't want to load you up with a lot of bad news, Rachel, but I have never had anyone recover from something as bad as this." He put his hand on her shoulder. "I will stay here until... something happens."

"I'll get you something to sleep on." She walked out of the room and down the stairs, as if in a dream, until Arturo asked how her mother was.

"I don't know, Arturo, I don't know. Would you please get a cot and take it up for the doctor?" She sat down on the last step then laid her head on her knees and cried. She stayed on the last step until the next morning. The doctor put his hand on her shoulder.

"Rachel, maybe you should go see her."

She stood in the doorway looking in the room and thinking how dark it was. The first thing her mother would do every morning would be to go around the house and pull all the curtains back to let in the daylight. She pulled back the curtains and looked at her mother. Had she always been that small or was it from the stroke? She brushed a few strands of gray hair from Adele's forehead.

"Ma." She sat on the bed. "I know you don't want to be like this. I don't want you to worry about me. If you want to go to Pa and Jacob, it's okay. Tell them I love them and will be seeing them on the bye and bye. I love you, but you can let go now." She kissed Adele and wiped tears from her eyes as she left the room.

Rachel sat in her mother's chair on the porch, staring at the clouds in the sky. She kept her mind busy looking for different shapes and trying not to think about her mother. The doctor stood inside the screen door for a moment before opening it and walking across the porch to where Rachel sat. She already knew what he was going to say.

Everyone in the valley attended the funeral. She told Arturo to take the crew and their families back to the ranch and she would join them later. She rode to the springs and sat on a large rock at the edge of the pond.

Chapter Twenty-nine
Nine Years Later

Rosa picked up the iron bar and hit the large metal triangle that hung on the pillar of the porch several times to let everyone know dinner was ready. She hurried to put the food on the table before everyone sat down in the chairs. Rachel was the last one to sit down. She reached across the table to stab a piece of meat with a fork, but Rosa slapped her hand.

"Mees Rachel, you know we are to say grace. How many time I must tell you?"

Rachel winked at Stony who was sitting across the table from her. "I forgot."

"Always you forgot." Rosa snorted then bowed her head. When no one spoke she opened her eyes and glared at the rest of them. They were all trying not to laugh.

"Stony, would you say grace this time?" Rachel finally said.

"Yes 'um."

After dinner they sat on the porch enjoying the evening breeze as it cooled the valley. Rachel watched the children of the ranch hands play in the yard. She remembered when she, Jacob, Birdie, and her brothers would play like that so long ago. Was it all a dream, she asked herself. It seemed so long ago that they were together and now she was the only one left.

"Mees, Rachel I go into town tomorrow. Is there something you like for me to do?"

"No Rosa, I don't need anything."

Rachel thought about what the ranch and the house would be like of Rosa wasn't there. After her mother died she spent most of the time away from the house. She slept in the tack room in back of the barn. She went into the house only to take care of ranch business and piled everything in stacks, and if they fell over she left them where they fell. She washed dishes only when she needed them and never learned how to cook.

Rosa, Arturo's aunt, came from Monterrey, Mexico. Her husband was a foreman on a ranch and died of cancer. She was evicted from the house they had lived in and came up north to visit relatives. Arturo was her sister's son, and she stopped to visit him. He took her into the house to talk to Rachel to see if she could live with him until she decided what she could do to support herself. Rachel gave the okay, and she moved in with Arturo. The following days she took it upon herself to clean the main house top to bottom. After the house was clean she gathered all of Rachel's clothes from the barn, washed them, and put them in the closets and dressers upstairs. Rachel took them back to the barn. Rosa gathered them up again and told Rachel to get her butt back to the house because that was where she belonged. Although neither one of them said a word it was understood that Rosa would be the housekeeper.

Three days later a horse and buggy turned onto the ranch property and stopped in front of the house. Two women sat in the front seat of the buggy with three women in the second seat. A large older woman sat in the third seat with a small child next to her.

"Ya'll gonna just stand there or ya'll gonna tell me if this is the O'Callahan ranch?" The woman in the last seat said to Rosa.

"Thees ees the O'Callahan ranch," Rosa answered back. To her knowledge no one Rachel knew had a buggy that fancy nor did they wear the kind of clothes the women in the buggy were wearing.

"Good," the woman said as she stepped off the buggy. "Damn it...my dress is caught. Lucille, would you please unhook my dress please?" The woman walked up the steps and sat in a chair. "Could you possibly tell Rachel O'Callahan that I need to have a word with her?"

Rosa wasn't quite sure what to make of the woman as she sat down.

"Well did you hear what I said? I need to talk to Rachel O'Callahan. Tell her that Miss Lillian needs to speak to her."

"Yes." Rosa walked down the stairs to find Rachel.

Rachel was lying on her stomach in a stall in the barn next to the milk cow. Her arm was inside the cow's uterus trying to turn the calf to the proper position for birth. She felt its head and legs but couldn't understand why the cow was having so much trouble giving birth.

"Well son of a bitch, no wonder she's having so much trouble, Arturo. She's got two of them in there. They're all tangled up. Let's see if I can get them straight."

She pushed her arm further inside the cavity. A few minutes later she slowly pulled a calf out by its hind legs. She gave it to Arturo to tear open the birth sack. Pulling the second calf out she ripped the sack and blew into the calf's nose to get it to breathe then placed it next to the cow.

"Next time, Maude, make it a little easier on your self and have just one calf."

"Mees Rachel." Rosa stood outside the stall.

"Yeah?"

"You have someone to see you."

"Who?" Rachel shut the gate on the stall.

"I don't know."

"What do they want?" Rachel grabbed a pitchfork to toss hay into the feed bucket for the cow.

"I don't know."

"If it's a peddler I don't want to talk to him."

"No peddler."

"Then who is it, Rosa? I don't have time to see anyone

now."

"A bawdy woman."

"Who?"

"A bawdy woman, Mees Rachel."

Rachel leaned on the edge of the pitchfork. "What the hell would a bawdy woman be doing out here?"

"I don't know, but there's one—a Miss Lillian in the parlor asking to see you."

"I'll be there as soon as I get cleaned up."

In the tack room where she had slept until Rosa showed up, she poured water from a jar into a pipe to prime a pump then pumped water into the wash basin. She stopped washing herself a couple of times to look in the mirror and wonder what a bawdy woman would be doing at the ranch. A few times in the last couple of years she had been to Virginia City to visit a bawdy house, but nothing unusual had happened. The women were nice, and it was easy to enjoy their company, but she had always paid the bill and never got into a fracas with anyone, so what would a bawdy woman be doing at the ranch?

Rachel stood outside the door of the parlor looking at the woman. She didn't recognize her from the bawdy houses she had visited. I guess I'll never know until I go in, she said to herself as she walked into the room.

"May I help you?" Rachel could tell the woman was surprised when she saw her.

Miss Lillian stared at Rachel for a long time before speaking. "Well lordy, you are just as I was told. I thought it to be a bit of a stretch but lordy lordy."

Rachel wasn't sure what to make of the woman and her talk.

"Please forgive me. I am Miss Lillian from Virginia City. I own a boarding establishment and a refreshment parlor there."

"I guess you would," Rachel said.

"I should start by saying that we have a mutual friend."

"We've never met before, have we?" Rachel wondered

which house Miss Lillian owned that she had visited.

"No, I must say we haven't, but I can see that is my loss." Rachel blushed.

"Do you know a woman by the name of Birdie Perez?"

The look on her face told Miss Lillian the answer.

"Do you know where she is?"

"No, I don't. I made a big mistake a while back, and that's why I am here now. I need to rectify my actions in the past." She walked to the door. "If you would excuse me for a moment, I have to get something from the buggy, then I can explain everything to you."

Rachel wondered what the woman was up to. "Yes."

After Miss Lillian left Rachel walked around the room wondering if the woman could tell her where Birdie was so she could bring her home. She heard the door open then the woman said, "Lucille, you stay here with her. I'll be back in a moment." Miss Lillian walked into the parlor. "I really think you should sit down."

Rachel looked at Lillian, wondering what in the hell was going on. She sat down thinking that if she was to find Birdie then she had to do what the woman wanted.

"Lucille, bring the child here to me."

Lucille walked to the doorway of the parlor and stopped. She was holding the hand of a little girl. Lillian took the hand of a little girl and led her into the parlor. "This child belongs to you."

"What in the hell is going on?" Rachel jumped up from the chair. "I don't have any children. I am certain that I should know that."

"Please allow me to explain why I have brought this child to you."

"What...you want to leave this unfortunate child with me to get her weight off your conscious mind?"

Lillian knew it would be hard to convince Rachel, but she had to try and make her understand. She had to take care of a debt she owed, and if it took everything she had then she would get the child to where it belonged.

"This is Birdie's daughter."

"This child has blue eyes. Birdie is Indian, and Indians don't have blue eyes. This can't be Birdie's child."

"If the father is a Swedish man she can. I can attest that her father was Swedish because I was at Birdie's wedding and at this child's birth."

Rachel knew she should tell the woman to go. The memory of Birdie as a little girl raced through her mind, and she closed her eyes hoping the memory would disappear. When she opened her eyes the same picture appeared, but she was looking into the eyes of the little girl.

"Might I ask that my associates outside with my buggy please be allowed in? It is terribly hot and unbearable on them."

"Yes. I will have Rosa bring some lemonade for you," Rachel said.

"This, of course, is Lucille." Lillian introduced the women as they walked into the parlor. "This is Carrey and Wanda and Leeann and Ethel."

"Please sit down," Rachel said.

"They knew nothing about the child until I looked for her and found her on the reservation in Wyoming."

"Yeah, we thought she was a bit daft traipsing all over the state of Wyoming looking for a little girl," Lucille said.

"We could have bankrolled ourselves a couple of times over if not for her." Carrey pointed at the girl.

"Oh be quiet, you two. We have a good thing in Virginia City, now so hush up."

Lillian picked up the girl and put her on her lap. "Come here, darlin. Didn't I tell you that I would make good my promise to you?" Lillian pointed at Rachel. "That is your new mother."

"You just can't assume that I will take her," Rachel said. "I don't have time for a little child, especially one that I am not sure of where she came from. How do I know that you just don't want to get her out of your hair?"

"I have her birth papers in my satchel." Lillian motioned at the door. "Carey, please be a dear and get them for me. I got them from the town recorder in Crawford's Landing up near Canada. I know this all sounds like a lot of bull, but please hear me out. I think you will come to see that she belongs here with you."

Rachel studied the woman while listening to what she had to say. She didn't want to believe what the woman was saying, but something was telling her to listen. "Okay, I will let you finish talking, but that doesn't mean that I will take the child when you leave."

"Fair enough," Lillian said. She cradled the girl in her lap and continued to speak. "I'll start from where I first met Birdie up in Crawford's Landing. I was working in a saloon when she came in looking for work. The owner didn't want any Indians around so he told her no, but I could tell that she weren't like the other Indians. She talked real good and carried herself with dignity. She didn't back down when one of the miners accused her of stealing a dollar from him. She told him she worked for her keep and didn't need to steal to get his money. He smashed a bottle against a table and threatened to cut her for her insolence, but she stood her ground. Frank the piano player found the dollar on the floor and gave it to him. When he took the dollar Birdie asked him for an apology. He left without apologizing, and I talked the owner onto letting her be my maid.

She cooked my meals and cleaned my apartment above the saloon everyday then she would go back across the border into Canada to the Indian camp at night. I had acquired some books from a few of my gentlemen friends, and she would take some with her to read. I never learned to read so she took it upon herself to teach me. Well I ain't no scholar, but at least now I know how to read." She picked up the glass with the lemonade and sat it back down on the table. "You wouldn't happen to have a bit of brandy would you? The lemonade is very tasty, but I need something with a little bit more of a kick to it, if you don't mind."

Rachel opened the wall cabinet, gave each woman a

glass, then poured brandy in each glass. Lillian swallowed the brandy in one gulp and held the glass out for more. Rachel poured some more into the glass and set the bottle on the table.

"Thank you sweetheart, some people aren't quite used to lemonade," Lillian said as she filled the glass to the top. "She worked for me for about eight months then he showed up. He being Ernst Van Eerden." She rolled her eyes and fanned her breast with her hand. "Why he was the most handsomest man and owned the largest gold mine on the border. Every woman in Crawford's Landing, married or not, wanted him and chased him unmercifully. One night I had convinced him to join me for dinner in my suite, and we were getting along fine until Birdie announced that dinner was ready. Well let me tell you that when he saw her he fell head over heels in love with her right then and there."

She drank the brandy and poured some more. "Lord, he chased her around town for months. I couldn't understand why she was so reluctant and trying her best to discourage him, but he was relentless. He built a large house outside of town with crystal chandeliers, the finest lace for the windows, and good solid oak furniture throughout the house and gave it all to her. After all that she still went back every night to Canada. He brought her flowers everyday when he wasn't working his mine. He even brought a matched pair of horses all the way from Kentucky just for her. I guess he finally wore her down because she just gave up and accepted his hand in marriage.

"It was a marriage like I have never seen before or since. He left money at the saloon after the ceremony and the whole town celebrated for days. They didn't come down from the house for three weeks. He, of course, went back to work at his mine, and she came back to work for me. He got mad and said that he didn't want his wife being no maid, but she told him that she would do what she damned well pleased."

Rachel smiled at the statement and remembered how stubborn Birdie had always been.

"He seemed to like her grit so he left her alone to do what she wanted. He spent longer days at the mine when he found out she was carrying his baby. He wanted to get all the gold out of the vein so they could leave Crawford's Landing for Pennsylvania. His family was there and he wanted to take her and the baby away from the lawlessness of the mining towns. One evening when he didn't return from the mine like he said he would she went out looking for him. She found him alongside the path to the mine where he had been bushwhacked. She buried him next to the house and lived there until the county assessor filed notice to take the house."

Rachel jumped when Lillian slammed the glass on the table after drinking the contents.

"God damned thieves. Seems they made a law after Ernst's death that Indians couldn't own property in the township and with her husband dead she had to leave. I told her that she could stay with me and we would get a lawyer man and find out what was going on. After the birth of this precious little thing things got real crazy." She tapped the side of her head as she spoke. "Seems Ernst was a lot smarter then we give him credit for."

She put the girl on the floor and walked around the room pouring brandy for the other women. "We all knew Ernst had left town for about a week after he found out he was to be a papa, but no one knew where he went, not even Birdie. Apparently he didn't trust a lot of people in town so he went to the territorial seat of government and had everything he owned put in a trust for the baby.

"Whoever killed him knew that with Birdie being Indian she couldn't have a claim on his mine so it would be fair game for anyone else to put a claim on it. The ink on them new claim papers hadn't even dried when a notice appeared in the assessor's office that all of Ernst's holdings belonged to his baby. Birdie went back to the house and two months later the baby was born.

"The birth was a bit difficult and the doctor didn't give the child a good chance of making it, but she has the spunk of her mother and here she is. When it came time to give the child a name Birdie said the name would be Rachel. This child is named after you." Lillian stopped talking to watch Rachel's response. "It was for sure that at the time I couldn't for the life of me understand why she gave the child that name. Ernst had wanted to name it after his father if it was a boy and his mother if it was to be a girl."

She emptied the bottle of brandy and set it down on the table. Rachel got another bottle from the cabinet and filled the glasses for all the women.

"Good brandy makes one's tongue loose to talk a lot, don't you think?" Lillian said.

Rachel set the bottle in front of Lillian. "Not unless you don't want to."

"You are a gracious host. Ladies, let's give her a toast."

The women all held up their glasses to Rachel.

"I thank ye for the hospitality," Carrey said.

"Hear hear," the others responded.

Lillian poured a glass and drank half of it. "Let's see...oh yeah...Birdie and me got real close during the following months and she told me about you and her and why she didn't want anything to do with Ernst. I thought it a down right miracle that she was still alive with all that she had been through. She did worry that you wouldn't want her because of what she had done with all those men. I told her that what she had been through was different. She said that women like her aren't respectable. She hoped that you'd find someone else that would be better for you. She married Ernst hoping to forget about you and the past."

Lillian walked to the window and pulled back the curtain to look outside. She didn't want Rachel to see the tears in her eyes. "Things got real crazy from then on. Birdie had custody of all of Ernst's holdings because of the child. As long as she had that baby no one could touch the claim. She got threats on the life of the baby and herself but she didn't back down—not until someone set the house on fire with her and the baby still in it. She decided to go down to Montana. She asked me to go with her, and the town was getting a little wild even for me so I left with her." Lillian wiped tears away from her eyes. "We were three days out when we were stopped by a cavalry troop. The lieutenant in charge said he was looking for the widow of Ernst Van Eerden. She told him that she was his widow then he told her that by decree of the commandant of the territory she had to give the child of Ernst to him. Someone had gone to Fort Kearney and filed adoption papers for the baby. Seems that if a child is half white and half Indian it can be taken from the Indian mother if the family of the white father wants it. She refused to give up the baby so they took it right out of her arms." She looked at Rachel. "They just snatched that child right out of her arms. She ran after the soldiers for a ways until one of them took aim at her and fired. He only grazed her leg, but it did knock her down. She didn't move from that spot the rest of the day or night. She just sat there swaying back and forth. I tried to get her to come back to camp, but I guess they finally broke her spirit."

"No one deserves to be treated like that, especially her." Lillian took a small linen cloth from her bosom and dabbed her eyes with it. "The next morning, without so much as a word, she packed the wagon and we started our for Bozeman. Two days later we arrived, and I looked up a saloon keeper I knew and he gave me a suite. I thought it would be like before, but she started to see to the men. I tried to get her not to, but it was no use. Having that child taken away from her was the last straw for her, and I think she just gave up on everything. She started drinking and carousing with the men. They got into fights over her. Real bad fights. Sid the owner told me that if I couldn't handle her then we would have to leave his establishment. I told her that if she didn't come to her senses then she would have to leave. She left that very night going I don't know where.

"One thing I can say is that she never stopped loving you. Even if she believed you wouldn't want her, she still loved you. In her mind that child was her last connection to you, and when they took it away they destroyed her." She sat back on the chair. "I stayed at Bozeman for six more months or so then I moved to Missoula. That's where I met all of these fine young ladies." She waved her hand in the air. "I seen one of the miners from Crawford's Landing, and we started talking about the old times. He asked me if I knew what happened to the Van Eerden baby. I told him what I knew, and he said he had heard that it was up on the Bitterroot reservation. He said that the county assessor and his wife had adopted the baby and when they got their hands on the mine claim they reneged on the adoption and sent the baby off to the reservation.

"I made myself a vow that I would find that baby and get her to where she belonged. It took me near two years, but with a hundred dollars to the Indian agent I got her. I know it's her because of her father's blue eyes. I tried to find Birdie, but she seems to have fallen off the face of the earth. I know that you'd agree that no child belongs with me the way I live. She belongs with her mother or with the one her mother really loved and that is with you."

Lillian shrugged her shoulders and looked at the other women when Rachel picked up the brandy bottle and left the parlor.

Rosa had been standing outside the room listening to the conversation. "She just thinking." She picked up the girl. "It be nice to have a young one in the house."

Rachel walked across the yard to the orchard gate. Leaning against it she raised the bottle and took a drink. She had finally convinced herself that Birdie wouldn't ever be back then this bawdy woman shows up with a little girl claiming that it was Birdie's. Should she believe what the woman had said? Maybe it was just a way to palm off an unwanted waif on her. But why would the woman come all the way out to the ranch? She knew of two childless homes in the valley that would jump at a chance to have a little girl. She thought of the way the girl looked at her. That was the same way Birdie had looked at her ever since she could remember. The only difference was the blue eyes. She took another swallow from the bottle. Maybe if she couldn't have Birdie she could at least have something that was part of her. Maybe it was Birdie's child, then again maybe it wasn't. She walked back to the house thinking she must be a fool for believing a story like that.

Chapter Thirty

Rachel stopped the wagon in front of the mercantile. Rosa took the basket of eggs from under the seat and walked into the store. Rachel followed her carrying a basket of peaches then returned to the wagon to get the milk canisters and set them in front of the counter.

"May I help you?" Sedwick the clerk stepped down from the ladder he had been on.

"We have eggs, peaches, and milk for the store," Rosa said to him as she tapped Rachel's arm. "Do you think Rachel would like a new dress for school?"

"You spoil that child," Rachel said.

"Not as much as you do."

Rachel laughed. "Yeah, I think she would like that."

"No, the blue would look better on her."

"Okay, buy what you need then. I have to see Mr. Grossman for some seed."

Rachel drove the wagon behind the livery stable then helped the stable hand put the sacks of seed in the wagon.

"Well well, we meet again." Major Wilson threw last sack on the wagon. "Have you thought about my proposal?"

"No, I haven't. I've had other things on my mind." She slammed the tail gate shut and locked it.

"See there, if you had a man to help you then your mind would be clear."

"My mind is perfectly clear, major, and I don't need any man to help me."

"If you change your mind you know where to find me."

"Humph," Rachel snorted.

"By the way, you wouldn't be planning on keeping that Indian kid, would you?"

"Whatever I plan to do is none of your business."

"You know a lot of people in this valley don't want any Indians around them, even if they are young un's."

"I really don't care what anyone in this valley thinks. I'll live my life my way, and they can live theirs the way they want."

He slapped his gloves against his leg. "I just hope that I don't have to come to the ranch for legal purposes."

"If you do you better bring your whole goddamned fort. You're not gonna take anyone from my ranch without a fight. Now if you'll excuse me I have better things to do than stand here jawing with you." She walked into the livery stable office and slammed the door.

"Bitch," the major said to the sergeant. "She's gonna need my help sooner than she thinks."

Rachel stopped in front of the mercantile to get Rosa and drove the wagon out of town back to the ranch. A year had passed since Lillian had left little Rachel at the ranch. Rachel couldn't believe how much she had become attached to her. Every day she could see the mannerisms that reminded her of Birdie, or did she just want to make herself believe it? Either way, just let the major try and take her away.

"What did you say, Rachel?" Rosa asked.

"Nothing. I was just thinking out loud."

"Something worry you, huh?"

"Yeah, I saw the major at the livery stable, and he said something about little Rachel."

"He won't take her away, will he?"

"Not if I can help it," she chucked the reins to get the horses up to a trot, "and certainly not without a fight.

At the main gate to the ranch Rachel stopped the wagon. "Do you smell that?"

"What?" Rosa asked.

"Look over there. There's a fire to the east."

"Oh yes, I see it now."

One of the ranch hands rode up to the wagon. "Rachel, Arturo sent me to get you. There's a fire out on the eastern meadow. It's growing and headed to the southwest."

"Let's get to the house, Rosa, and I'll get Jester and go help the men. You and the others get supplies ready and you can bring them in the wagon."

Rachel rode out to the East Meadow and stopped Jester on a ridge. Some of the men were slapping at the ground with blankets to knock out the fire while some of them had ropes tied to both ends of logs dragging them to clear the brush from the fire's path. The wind gusts kept blowing ashes and embers across the area cleared out by the logs. She watched as the fire slowly encircled the men and decided to get them out of the meadow. Arturo met her at the end of the fire line.

"Get the men and get the hell out of here," she yelled to Arturo.

"We've got to stop it now. If it continues on this path it will burn the ranch houses," he yelled at her.

"Then we need to make a stand before it gets there. The wind is too fast right now and everything we do here isn't working. It's too dangerous for the men to stay here. I'm afraid it's going to circle them and they won't be able to get out. We'll get back down there and get ready for it."

She rode back to the house and ran into the kitchen. "Rosa, get what you need and get it to the root cellar. The fire is coming this way, and you don't have a lot of time. The god damned wind is starting to howl and blow this way. Where is little Rachel?"

"She's down at Arturo's place with Felina. I told her to stay there until I come back to get her."

"Tell Felina to put all of the children in the cellar and tell them to stay there. Tell everyone else to get prepared for a fight. I'm going to put men on the plows and have them circle the property as much as they can. Arturo will put two men on

Mason Valley Ranch

the pump to fill the tower as much as possible if we need a fire brigade. We'll need every one that can carry a bucket."

"Yes." Rosa ran out the door.

Rachel ran to the barn and opened all the stalls. She didn't try to keep any of the horses in the pen. She just wanted them to get to out of the barn. They could round them up later after the fire.

"Rachel, it's coming up over the ridge." Arturo ran into the barn.

"Son of a bitch." She ran out of the barn. "The god damned wind isn't helping us at all."

"I'm going to open all of the gates to all of the pens and let the livestock go," Arturo said.

"I'm right behind you," she said running behind him.

"There's fire at the back of the haystacks," a ranch hand yelled from across the yard.

"Stony, get some men and meet me there." Rachel grabbed a bucket and ran to the back of the barn. The last stack of hay bales was on fire and the third had already started smoldering as the red embers fell on it.

"We can't save those," Rachel shouted as she dipped the bucket in the water trough. "Pour water on the first two. We've got to save these no matter what."

"Rachel, the barn is on fire!" Rosa yelled at her.

Rachel knew they needed the hay, but it would be more important to save the barn for the winter. "Arturo, leave two men to work the hay and take everyone to the barn."

All of the men followed her to the barn. The woman had already formed a line from the pump to the barn for a bucket brigade. Rosa directed the women to pump and fill the buckets while the men threw the water on the fire. If they could keep the fire at the bottom of the barn and not on top then they could save it.

"The roof...it's on the roof!" Arturo yelled.

Rachel looked up like everyone else to see the roof engulfed in flames. She knew it would be useless to try and save it. "Everyone get back."

The bucket brigade wouldn't stop. They were trying to fight it as much as they could.

Rachel ran along the line shouting at them. "It's no use, you will get hurt. Get away now."

"We have to save it," Stony said.

"Stony, it's no use and you know it." She grabbed the bucket from his hand. "Get everyone away from here before someone gets hurt."

He didn't want to stop, but he also knew she was right. The barn was totally engulfed in flames, and they had to save the other buildings.

"Get away," he yelled choking on the smoke. "Get back to the houses and save them."

Four hours later Rachel stood in the middle of the yard looking at the damage. The barn was gone, along with the milk house and all of the pens for holding the horses and other livestock. The wind had shifted and the fire singed the side of the main house, but it was intact. The other houses for the hired hands had also escaped the fire. She would have to build a new barn before winter set in and that would use most of the money she had. They had managed to save two hay stacks, but it wouldn't be enough to feed the cattle through the winter. She would have to sell more of the cattle than she had planned this year and that would make it harder to get calves in the spring. Without the calves the herd would be small next year, making it hard to get money for rebuilding the ranch.

"Rachel, I have someone here that you need to talk to," Arturo said as he walked up to her. "This is Orville from the Lazy J Ranch to the east of us. He came to help us, and he told me something I think you should know."

"What?"

"I just want to say how sorry I am for all this," Orville said.

"Uh huh."

"I...uh...I was on line duty fixing fence along our properties this morning and I saw two men riding like hell on fire along the ditch road. I was wondering what would make them ride like that, then I saw the smoke on the hill. I cain't for sure say what started it, but them two fella's was surely in a hurry to get out of there before it got going good. It looked like they were wearing the blue coats like the cavalry men wear, but I couldn't swear to it. I rode back to the Lazy J and got as much help as I could. I just wish we could have been here sooner to save the barn."

"You were a big help with the houses and all the other things, and I thank you. Tell the other men that I appreciate their help."

"Yessum. If you need help rounding up the livestock we'll be most happy to help."

"Thank you. I probably will need some help with that. Arturo, would you take care of that for me? I have to get to the house and see what can be done about the other things."

Chapter Thirty-one

The train stopped at Wabuska long enough for Rachel and two cowboys to disembark. She waited for the last car to pass so she could walk to the stable to get Jester. It was faster to ride the train to Virginia City then ride all day and half the night on horseback. Mathews, the attorney, had sent a letter requesting her presence at the courthouse regarding the lien against the ranch. He also wanted to talk to her in person about the fire after she sent a letter to him. The judge was in bed with the gout and had to reschedule everything. It cost her a night at a boarding house, but at least for now the ranch was still hers.

She rang the bell outside the door of the stable to get Jester and Luke the big black dog. She had planned to use the old wagon road that followed the river to the ranch but decided instead to stop at Miss Nell's restaurant for something to eat. The sun was setting behind the mountain when she left the restaurant with two hours to the ranch. Passing the alley next to the old grist mill she heard a crashing sound and stopped to see what was going on. A woman was fighting, trying to get away from two men. Rachel took her shotgun out of the scabbard and walked into the alley. One of the men hit the woman with his fist. When she fell to the ground the second man pulled her hands up above her head and tied them to a post. He then sat on a box to watch as the other man lay on top of her. Rachel placed the barrel of the gun against his temple.

"Get off of her."

"What the hell?" the man said.

"I said, get off of her."

"This ain't none of your business," the man sitting on the box said.

Rachel cocked the shotgun. "This is the last time I will tell you to get off of her."

He pushed himself up to his knees.

"Now back up."

He reached down to pull his pants up.

"Leave them down."

"I cain't stay here with my pants like this, it ain't decent." He tried again to pull them up.

She pressed the barrel into his temple. "You didn't seem to care about that while you were having your way with her, did you?"

"That ain't the same."

"It is to me."

"Who the hell are you?" he bellowed.

"Never mind who I am."

The man looked to his right into the darkness. "Bailey, are you gonna help me or not?"

Bailey sat on the box looking at the big black dog standing about three feet in front of him. "Looks like you're doing alright so far." He was trying to stay calm so the dog would stay where it was.

"Bailey, I'm gonna kick your ass for leaving me like this." He looked at Rachel. "We don't mean no harm. My brother and me are couple of cowboys been traveling for a spell and stopped for some grub and a little bit of excitement. Besides, look at her, she ain't nothing but a damned Indian."

Rachel lowered the gun then pushed the barrel between his legs. "See if this doesn't get you a little bit excited."

He watched the barrel slide between his legs then looked at her. "No!"

The roar of the shotgun drowned out his voice as he yelled. He reached down to feel between his legs and saw blood, then grabbed himself with both hands. He stiffened up and fell on his side, rolling back and forth on the ground.

"You bitch, you shot my balls off. Bailey, she shot my balls off. Do something damn it, she shot my balls off."

Bailey sat on the box watching him roll around while keeping an eye on the dog. Rachel turned the shotgun to Bailey.

"You have any business with me?"

Bailey swallowed hard. "No, I don't rightly think I do."

"I think your brother needs a doctor." She watched him roll around.

"Ah, yessum, it appears that way."

"Are your horses nearby?"

"Yessum they are." He pointed to the other end of the alley.

"Why don't you go get them and get him to a doctor?"

"Well ma'am, I don't think he's gonna be able to ride right about now."

Rachel cocked the shotgun. "I don't care if he can ride or not. If you don't get him out of my sight real soon then you won't be riding either."

"Yes ma'am." He jumped down from the box squeezing his body between Rachel and Luke. She watched the man as he rolled back and forth moaning.

"Here I come ma'am...don't shoot." Bailey held his hands out in front of his body for her to see. He tried to pick up his brother. "Come on, Hadley, let's get on out of here."

"Don't touch me. I cain't move, god damned it. She shot my balls clean off." Hadley pushed his brother's hand away from him.

"I know, I saw it, but if you don't get up she's gonna shoot mine off too." He jerked Hadley's arm. "Now come on."

"Oow...I cain't ride no horse, you numbskull."

"Well then walk cause I ain't gonna get shot." Bailey started to mount his horse.

"Okay, okay, hold your hands out," Hadley moaned.

Bailey clenched his fists together and hoisted Hadley into his saddle.

"Son of a bitch," Hadley yelled as he hit the saddle.

"Shut the hell up, god damned it. I told you that one day you'd get into a peck of trouble. We're gonna find a doctor, so just shut up."

After Bailey led the horses out of the alley Rachel bent down to see if she could help the woman. It was dark in the alley, but she knew who the woman was.

"Come on Luke, let's take Birdie home."

Chapter Thirty-two

Rosa knocked lightly on the door several times, waiting for the okay to enter. When no answer came she turned the knob and pushed the door open.

"I have something for you to eat. It's been two days you are here with nothing to eat. You need to build your strength." She set the tray on the table then fluffed the pillows and pulled the sheets up on the bed.

"Don't bother. I'm not staying," Birdie said as Rosa watched her.

Rosa tossed the quilt over the bed, ignoring Birdie's statement. "You need to eat. This is my best soup."

Birdie looked at the food. She was hungry, and it had been a while since she had eaten anything. She pushed the spoon back and forth with her fingers thinking about the last time she ate with this silverware. She sat down in the chair.

"Ees there anything else I can get you?" Rosa asked.

"No...yes. Where are my clothes?"

"Mees Rachel tells me to burn them."

"Burn them, why?"

"She says they rags. She says to bring you new clothes." Rosa walked to the door. "I come back with new clothes."

Birdie was almost finished with the soup when Rosa returned.

"You like more? I have plenty more."

Birdie didn't answer.

Rosa put the clothes on the bed. "Mees Rachel says you should like to wear this."

"Does Mees Rachel tell everyone what they want around here?" Birdie said mocking her.

"No, she only wants the best for you. She tells me that. I take care of you for her. All time I am here she waits for you to return. She very lonely for you. She very worried for you. She stays here for two days waiting for you to get better. I tell her I take care of you and make her go do chores. I tell her that you are awake now."

"No don't," Birdie snapped back. "I'm leaving as soon as I get those clothes on."

"But why?" Rosa asked.

"I don't belong here anymore."

"You belong here as much as I do," Rachel said as she walked into the room.

"I go now." Rosa squeezed between Rachel and Birdie and closed the door behind her.

"Are you okay?" Rachel asked.

Birdie turned away from Rachel. "Why did you bring me here?"

"This is your home. This is where you belong."

"You shouldn't have brought me here. You should have left me."

"Left you where? In that alley?" Rachel stepped further into the room. "You belong on this ranch with me."

"Not anymore." Birdie stepped back from the table.

"Birdie, I'm not going to do anything to hurt you."

Birdie hit the table with her hand. "I have to leave, Rachel. I can't stay."

"Why Birdie?" Rachel folded her arms.

"Because...because...." Birdie looked up at the ceiling trying to find words to make Rachel understand.

"Just tell me why you can't stay where you were born and grew up."

"Because whores like me don't live in respectable houses, Rachel."

"You're not a whore, Birdie."

"You don't know that."

"I know you."

"What you want is in the past, Rachel, and that will never be again. The best thing you can do for yourself is to let me go back to where you found me."

"You know I can't do that, Birdie."

"You wouldn't say that if you knew what I've done. I've been with men, Rachel, lots of men. I've killed and robbed people. I am not the same person that left here years ago."

Rachel didn't say anything.

"What if I told you that I don't love you any more?"

"I can't and I won't believe that," Rachel said.

"Well it's true. And the sooner you let me go away from here the better it will be for both of us."

"Birdie, if you leave then I will follow you. I lost you once, and I'm not going to lose you again."

"You won't leave your precious ranch."

"The hell I won't. I'll leave this ranch and everything on it to be with you."

"You're a fool, Rachel."

"Say what you want, but it won't change my mind."

Birdie grabbed the front of the nightgown she was wearing and ripped it apart, letting it fall to the ground.

Rachel looked down at the floor.

"Look at me," Birdie said.

Rachel didn't look up.

"God dammned it, I said look at me," Birdie yelled. "You think you're in love with me? What you are in love with is a person from the past. Not someone that looks like this." Rachel watched Birdie turn around.

"This is the body of a whore, Rachel, not the body someone wants to love."

"It doesn't matter, Birdie."

"Maybe you don't love me," Birdie said. "Maybe you want me for your very own whore. Is that it?"

"Stop it, Birdie."

"Maybe you just want to see for yourself how a whore satisfies the men. Is that what you want?" Birdie grabbed Rachel's belt and unbuckled it. "Shall I get down on my knees or maybe I should lay down on the bed. Do you prefer me on my back or my stomach?"

"Stop it, Birdie."

Birdie walked to the dresser and turned away from Rachel as she put her hands on the top. She looked at Rachel in the mirror. "Do you prefer that I should just spread my legs like this?"

"I said stop it, Birdie."

"That's what a whore does, Rachel, and that is what I am." She looked at herself in the mirror and slammed her fist against it, shattering the glass. "A god damned whore."

Shoving everything on the dresser to the floor, she grabbed for the knife on the table and put it to her throat. Rachel lunged across the table, but the blade drew blood before she could knock it away. They wrestled for the knife, knocking the table over as they fought. Birdie didn't have the strength to continue fighting and stopped when Rachel pinned her to the floor.

"Why can't you just leave me be, Rachel? Just leave me be."

Rachel wrapped her arms around Birdie. "Because you belong here and you know it."

Rosa walked up and down the hall in front of the room several times. She hadn't heard any sound for quite a while and was concerned. Surely one of them would have opened the door if something bad had happened. What if both of them were hurt, then neither of them could get help. She couldn't stand it any longer and slowly turned the door knob. Peeking through the small crack in the door she saw Rachel leaning against the wall, asleep, with Birdie's head on her shoulder.

Chapter Thirty-three

Rosa poured the last bucket of hot water into the tub and stirred it with her hand. She held up a small bell.

"Just ring if you need anything."

Birdie sat on the edge of the bed wrapped in a blanket. She had woken up when Rosa knocked on the door to check on her but didn't remember getting into bed. The lavender scent of the water brought back memories of her mother. She stepped into the warm water and leaned back. After the bath she put on the clothes Rosa had placed for her on the bed. Combing her hair she walked to the window. She watched Rachel and the ranch hands building a new barn. She also noticed a little girl who followed Rachel everywhere she went.

Rachel led some horses into the pen next to the barn. Little Rachel pushed the gate to close it. They were walking to the back of the house when Rachel noticed Birdie was sitting in one of the rockers on the front porch.

"Tell Rosa I'll be there in a little while, okay?" Rachel said.

"Okay." Little Rachel ran into the house.

"That little girl, is she one of the hired hands' children?" Birdie asked as Rachel stepped up on the porch.

"No, she's mine."

Birdie had a surprised look on her face. Rachel could tell that Birdie was trying to figure it out.

"Aren't you going to say anything about it?" she asked.

"Why should you care about what I have to say?" Birdie snapped back.

"I happen to care quite a lot about what you have to say. I always have and always will."

Birdie walked to the end of the porch and sat on the rail. "I do find it hard to believe that you of all people would have relations with a man."

"I didn't." Rachel sat next to Birdie. "Besides, if I really thought it would be to the good I could bring myself to have relations with a man."

"Not you, Rachel. I remem...," Birdie stopped. "I remember how you were and it would be most surprising even to know that you would lay down next to a man for any reason."

Rachel rubbed the rail with her hand. "I have wants and needs, Birdie, just like everyone else."

"I expect you would, but no matter how dire the need you wouldn't be with a man."

"I've been with some women." Rachel stood up and put her hands in the pockets of the denims she was wearing. "I visited some of the bawdy women in Virginia City. They were nice and very helpful, but it wasn't you. Finally it got to where I would visit and we would just talk. I told all of them about you, and try as they might they just couldn't be you."

Birdie thought about the last night they were together at the line shack. She turned her head to keep Rachel from seeing the tears in her eyes. She was crying not only for the past but for the future. She wanted so much to hold Rachel, but Rachel deserved so much better.

"I adopted her," Rachel said.

"I'm sorry, Rachel, what?" Birdie wiped tears from her eyes.

"I said that I adopted her. A woman came to the ranch three years ago and gave her to me."

"Why would a woman give a baby to you?"

"A woman that knew she let the mother of the baby down and was trying to make something that she messed up right. A woman that knew the mother of the baby would want it to be taken care of by someone that loved her."

Birdie walked back to the rocker.

"A woman named Miss Lillian from Crawford's Landing."

Birdie stopped but didn't turn around.

Rachel continued. "A woman who looked for months to find an Indian baby girl who was taken away from its mother because the father owned a gold mine. The father was killed for the mine, and the mother and baby were forced out of the home. The baby was taken away from its mother for adoption by a white couple only to be put on a reservation in Wyoming when the deed to the gold mine was in hand."

Birdie covered her face with her hands as Rachel spoke.

"A woman who told me that the baby's name is Rachel Van Eerden."

Birdie sat in the rocker.

"I know about everything, Birdie. I know about the mining and logging camps. I know about Canada and Crawford's Landing. I know about your husband and I know about the men." Rachel leaned against a pillar next to Birdie. "I thought I'd never see you again, and when Miss Lillian came here with that child I had to believe it was yours."

"It can't be my baby." Birdie's voice was trembling. "My baby had blue eyes."

Rachel pointed at the house. "That little girl in there has the beautiful face of her mother and the deepest blue eyes of her father."

"It isn't true, Rachel. It can't be true."

"I don't know why providence turns certain things the way it does, but somehow after all his time we wound up here together and that's the way is should be." Rachel dropped to her knees in front of the rocker. "I love you, Birdie, and if it takes the rest of my life to prove it to you then I will. If all I ever have is memories of the two of us together from the past then so be it. Just knowing you will stay here with me is all I want. I lost you once, and I can't do that again."

The screen door slammed against the wall as Little Rachel ran through it.

"How many times have I told you not to do that?" Rachel scolded her.

Little Rachel hung her head down.

"Come here, I want you to meet someone." Rachel motioned with her hand. "This is your...uh...this is...."

"Hello, my name is Birdie. What's your name?"

"Rachel."

"That's a very pretty name," Birdie said. "Could I please give you a great big hug?"

Little Rachel looked at Rachel to get approval.

"Go ahead."

Little Rachel let Birdie hold her for as long as she could stand still, then raced off the porch with Luke.

"Don't chase the chickens too much or they won't lay," Rachel shouted at them. She wrapped her hands around Birdie's. "Will you stay?"

Birdie liked the feel of Rachel's hands around hers. She watched Little Rachel play with Luke and thought of the many trials she had been through.

"If I can stay in my mother's house."

"I wish you'd stay here in the main house, but if that's what you want then that's the way it will be."

Chapter Thirty-four

Birdie led the horse into the stall and blocked the doorway with the poles in the temporary slots. She took off the saddle and bridles, threw some hay into the feed bin, and filled the bucket with water. The barn was almost finished except for the doorways on the stalls and planking on the lofts. The hay and alfalfa bales were stacked behind the barn waiting until the lofts could get finished during the winter. The cool air of autumn was coming into the valley, and it was imperative that they got the last of the alfalfa and hay cut and stored. The warm rays of the sun were being overtaken by the chill of the wind as it blew down the mountain. She rubbed her arms and shoulders as she walked to her house. It had been five months since Rachel brought her back to the ranch. She had stayed away from everyone for the first two months.

Everyday Rachel walked by the cabin on the way to the main house or the barn and never offered a word unless she was spoken to. A large yard separated the main house and barn. Birdie's cabin was the first structure to the east of the barn with the other cabins lined up along the canal road behind it. Rachel never asked her to help even though it was obvious that some things wouldn't get done before winter. The fire had been devastating to the feed supply. They spent the better part of two months searching for all the cattle and horses. Rachel had to trade half of the cattle herd to the other ranchers to get supplies and equipment to rebuild the barn the pens and out fences. Neighboring ranchers offered what hired hands they could spare to help rebuild the fences and raise the frame of the barn. Birdie spent the time on the small wooden porch of her cabin watching all the activity.

One of the hired hands fell off the roof of the barn and broke his leg. Rachel sat on the back of the supply wagon watching the dust cloud behind the buggy taking him to town to the doctor. She ran her hands through her hair and wondered when it was all going to stop. When would she be able to get things back in order? She was determined to make the ranch prosper, but how much more could she take before it would be useless? She didn't see Birdie walk up to the wagon.

"What do you want me to do?" Birdie said.

"Nothing."

"Tell me what you want me to do, Rachel."

Rachel hopped off the wagon and slammed the tail gate shut. "I don't have the barn finished and it's getting late in the fall. I don't have enough feed for the cattle even though I had to barter half of the herd for supplies. I'm brokered up to the hilt with everyone in town, and no matter what I do I can't get things right. It seems that everywhere I turn I get blocked. I can't keep the ranch if I can't raise cattle. I can't raise cattle if I can't grow feed. If I can't sell the cattle then I can't pay the notes. Can you do something about that? Hell, I might as well just quit fighting and put the ranch up on the auction block."

"Don't say that, Rachel."

"I might as well say it because it's beginning to look like that is what I will have to do."

"It will take some time, but you will overcome all this."

"And you would know that?" Rachel knew it was the wrong thing to say as soon as she said it. "I'm sorry, Birdie. I didn't mean to say that."

"Then why did you say it?"

"I don't know, Birdie." Rachel waved her hands in the air as she talked. "Why do the moon and sun come up in the east and go down in the west? If I could figure that out then I could give you the answer."

Birdie reached inside the wagon for a hammer and a sack of nails. "The barn isn't going to get finished by itself."

"No, I guess it isn't," Rachel said.

Three months later Birdie closed the door of the cabin to join the others in the main house for dinner.

"Birdie, would you say grace please?" Rosa said after she sat down.

"Me?" Birdie asked.

"Yes, I think it time for you." Rosa smiled at her.

It was the first time Rosa had asked her to say grace. She tried to remember the words that Adele said. When she finished she looked at Rosa. "I hope that was okay."

"Okay." Rosa said. "I get coffee pot now. Start passing around the food."

"Where is Rachel?" Birdie asked.

"She say she have something to do but for us to start eating." Rosa put the coffee pot in the middle of the table.

Dinner was almost over when Rosa noticed a flickering light in the mirror on the wall. She scooted her chair back and walked to the window. "Dios Mio! Mees Birdie, your house on fire."

"What?" Birdie said.

"Your house is burning on fire."

Birdie jumped up and looked out the window. She ran across the yard, hoping to get her things out of the cabin, but it was engulfed in flames.

"It's too late." Rachel grabbed her and held her away from the flames.

"I have to get my things out of there." Birdie struggled to get away from Rachel.

"Don't worry, they're over there." Rachel pointed to the barn. "I made sure everything was out."

"Are you okay? You didn't get burned or hurt did you?" Birdie asked Rachel.

"No, I'm not hurt."

After the cabin had been reduced to smoldering ashes Birdie walked to the barn to see what was left of her things. She wasn't sure what she would find, but hopefully Rachel was able to save most of her things. She was surprised to see everything she owned in the barn.

"How did you get all of my things out of there?"

"I carried them out," Rachel said. "Then I started the fire."

"What?" Birdie yelled. "Why in the hell did you burn down my house?"

"Because," Rachel folded her arms, "you belong over there in the main house with me."

"Who gives you the right to tell me where I am to live?" Birdie shouted at her.

"You know that I'm right."

"I belong where the hell I say I belong. I knew it was a mistake staying here with you." Birdie was shaking as she spoke. "God damn you, Rachel. You're just like all the rest of them. I'm leaving this damned place and I'm leaving you."

"Go ahead and leave if that's what you want." Rachel grabbed Birdie's arm. "That is what you want, isn't it? You don't care about the ranch or anyone on it."

"Why should I care about anyone, Rachel? It's only brought me grief and pain."

"Yeah, I guess you're right, Birdie. No one cares about you. Why should you care about this ranch? What would you know about pride and commitment?" Rachel released Birdie's arm. "Hell, you're just an Indian anyway."

Birdie slapped Rachel's face. "Don't you ever say that to me again, Rachel O'Callahan. Yes, I am an Indian and I am damned proud of it. I was born on this ranch, and I've worked just about as hard as anybody to keep it going. I plan to die on this ranch, and no one, not you, not the townspeople, or the damned government is going to make me leave this ranch again. Never." She spun around, almost knocking Rosa to the ground to walk back to the main house. Rachel watched her until she walked through the back door slamming it shut.

Rachel grinned at Rosa. "I think that went pretty well, don't you?"

"You burn up Mees Birdie's house then fight with her and think it funny. Mees Rachel, sometime you plenty loco." Rosa walked back to the house shaking her head.

Rachel watched the house until she saw the glow of a lamp in a window. She smiled as she walked toward the house. Of all the bedrooms Birdie could have picked to stay in she took the one next to hers.

Chapter Thirty-five

Sheriff Griffey stopped his horse at the gate to the Mason Valley Ranch. He didn't want to go onto the property because he didn't want to do what he came here to do. He remembered Sean and Adele O'Callahan and how they helped him get elected to the office. He missed Sean and his stories of his youth back east. He missed Adele because he took a more than friendly liking to her although she was married. He missed the apple pies she always made for him when they had to go to town. He missed the way she always touched his arm and kissed his cheek whenever she had to leave.

"I wonder if she might have taken a shine to me too," he said out loud to the horse. He took off his hat and wiped his brow. "I didn't come all the way out here just for the hell of it."

He tied the horse to a post and walked up the steps. Rosa stopped sweeping the porch when she saw him riding to the house.

"May I help you, sheriff?"

"I need to speak to Rachel."

"I get her for you." She propped the broom against the house walked down the steps and around the house.

Rachel walked up the steps. "Hello, Sheriff Griffey."

"Hello, Rachel. I see that you put up a new barn."

"Yeah, the fire last year burnt the old one down. I still got a few things to do inside, but at least the lofts and stalls are done now."

"Yeah, I heard about the fire. At least the house didn't get burned."

"No, thank goodness. It just scorched the other side a bit. We did lose most of the feed bales, the pens, and fence lines." Rachel rubbed the back of her neck. "It's just something else that has happened around here."

"I heard you leveraged some property to the north."

"Yeah, I had to get feed and supplies to rebuild. I leveraged half of the spring calves too. I figure that if I have three good years I'll be to the good if nothing else don't come up."

"I hope so for your sake." He scratched his beard.

"I know you didn't come out here for chit chat, so what do you need?"

"I…uh." He pulled an envelope from his shirt pocket. "I have a court order to place you under arrest."

"Arrest?"

"Is there anything you need to tell me about, Rachel?"

"Like what?"

"I don't know. Has anything happened on the ranch that I need to know about?"

"Nothing other than the things I've told you about."

"Well it doesn't make any sense to me either. The court of Yerington has issued this order for your arrest, and I am supposed to take you back to jail. I don't want to do that, and I need your promise that you will be in court on the fourteenth of October."

She took the summons from his hand and read it. "Okay, sheriff, I will."

"Does that name Hadley Corchoran mean anything to you?"

She shook her head no.

"Well, according to this," he took another piece of paper from his pocket, "you shot him. You shot him while he was in an alley in Yerington."

She remembered the men in the alley. "Yeah, I shot someone, but I didn't get his name."

"You want to tell me what happened?"

"I was on my way back to the ranch from Virginia City. I took the old wagon road to get to Miss Nell's place. When I was leaving town I saw two men accosting a woman in an alley. One of the men, I guess it was that Hadley fellow, was having his way with her and I told him to leave her alone. He wasn't very cooperative so I shot him to make him stop. I told the other man to take him to the doctor."

"Was it self defense?" the sheriff asked.

"No, but I got him away from her."

"It would help if you had that woman as a witness," the sheriff said. "Do you know who the woman was?"

"Yes, I do." Rachel thought about giving him Birdie's name then decided against it. "Do I have to tell you who she is?"

"If what you're saying is true then you should. It will help you a lot when you go to court." he said.

"It was me."

The sheriff turned around to see Birdie standing in the doorway.

"She was protecting me."

"You're Birdie Perez, aren't you?"

"Yes, I am."

"I heard that you were back. I guess the wire I answered a while back reached the right people."

Rachel wondered what they were talking about.

"What's going on?" Birdie asked.

"I have an arrest warrant for Rachel for attempted murder."

"Rachel didn't murder anyone," Birdie said.

The sheriff opened the door. "Make sure that you are at the courthouse on October fourteenth."

Birdie took the paper and read it. "What are you going to do?"

Rachel shrugged her shoulders. "There's not much I can do except go to the courthouse on October fourteenth."

"It's my fault. If you hadn't stopped that night this wouldn't be happening," Birdie said.

"Birdie, it could have been someone else in that alley and it wouldn't have made any difference. I would have done the same thing and I'd still have to go court."

Birdie took Rachel's hand. "I'm sorry. Rachel."

"It's not your fault, Birdie."

Birdie touched Rachel's cheek with her hand. Rachel put her hands around Birdie's waist to pull her closer. Little Rachel ran into the room and grabbed Rachel's arm.

"Mommy, come quick. The mare's foaling."

"Okay, honey, I'm coming." Rachel took a deep breath and looked back at Birdie as she left the room.

Chapter Thirty-six

The last stop for the V and T Railroad was at the depot in the north end of Virginia City. Rachel stepped off the railroad car and took the valise and her shotgun from Birdie before helping the other women down onto the platform.

"Where is the Star Hotel?" she asked the clerk behind the ticket window.

"Three blocks climb up the street to the west then south for four blocks," he answered.

They walked into the hotel and stopped at the front desk.

"We don't want no Indians in here." The clerk behind the desk slammed the sign register shut.

"She is with us," Rachel said.

"I don't care who she is with. She ain't going to stay here."

Rachel propped the barrels of the shotgun on the desk before she grabbed his shirt and pulled him halfway across the desk. "I am telling you that she is with us."

"No Rachel," Birdie said.

"This gentleman is going to open the register and you can sign us in," Rachel said.

"I don't want any trouble, Rachel," Birdie said.

"There isn't going to be any trouble, is there mister?" Rachel let go of his shirt.

"No ma'am." He straightened his collar opened the book and turned it around.

"Here." The man grabbed two keys and threw them on the desk. "You are two floors up."

"You and Little Rachel are in that room. Birdie and I are in this one," Rachel said to Rosa as she gave her the key. She looked at Birdie. "That is, if it's okay with you?"

"Do I have a choice?" Birdie asked.

"Yes, you do." Rachel unlocked the door and pushed it open.

Birdie knew there was only one bed in the room. She also knew Rachel had had plenty of opportunities to try something while they worked side by side on the ranch. Several times they had been out in the fields together with no one else around. She even began to wonder if Rachel cared for her anymore. It was like they had never known each other before she came back.

"It's okay with me." Birdie walked through the door.

Rachel put the valise on the bed. "I have to go see the attorney. Why don't you take Rosa and Little Rachel down to dinner and I'll catch up with you in a bit?"

"Okay."

Rachel could smell the scent of lavender as she walked up the steps to Mathews' office and knocked on the door. He jerked the door open.

"Oh, it's you. I didn't expect to see you until tomorrow at the courthouse."

"I need to talk to you about a few things." She sat in the chair in front if his desk.

"I can't think of anything we need to talk about. I thought that we pretty well covered everything in our correspondence." He shut the door.

"We talked about everything but payment to you for your services."

"We'll talk about that after the trial." He sat in his chair.

"We need to talk about it now in case I go to jail."

"Whoa, now Rachel, let's not get the horse before the buggy. I don't plan on you going to jail."

"I have to get things settled before hand just in case." She took an envelope out of her shirt pocket. "I want you to read and sign this."

"What is it?"

"It's what I'm going to pay you for your services. I don't have a lot of money."

He read the paper. "I can't sign this. It's your...."

Rachel interrupted him. "If I go to jail I need to know that someone I trust will keep the ranch in good stead."

"I won't take the ranch for payment." He dropped the paper on the desk. "Leave it to Birdie."

"I'd like to leave it to Birdie, but we both know that there are too many people that would stop it. She has had a rough go of things in her life, and she doesn't need my business to hamper her either."

"It wouldn't be right," he said.

"If I go to jail Birdie will be your foreman. She knows as much, if not more, than I do about the ranch. If I don't go to jail then I will be your foreman."

"I won't sign it," he said.

Rachel dipped the nib of his pen into the ink bottle and held it out for him. "Sign it or you won't be my attorney today or any other day."

He didn't want to take her ranch nor did he want to own a ranch. He was an attorney and didn't have a clue as to what happens on a ranch. He also knew he could never get her to change her mind. He took the pen from her. "You are a very determined woman."

She blew on the ink until it dried then folded the paper and put into her shirt pocket. "See you at the courthouse tomorrow."

Birdie sat in a chair at the window looking down at the street. She remembered the many times she and Rachel and their mothers would be in town to sell the butter and eggs or the fruit from the orchard. They would have lunch at the Traveler's Station House then take their time getting back to the ranch. When they were old enough to come to town on their own they would skip the lunch at the Traveler's Station and go out to the springs. It was so long ago that she wondered if it really happened.

She wondered where Rachel went. She also thought about what would happen when it came time to go to bed. She wanted so much to lie next to Rachel and feel her arms around her. So many times she wanted to reach out to Rachel only to give up because she was so ashamed.

Rachel opened the door half way. "Is it alright to come in?"

Birdie turned in the chair. "Yes."

Rachel closed the door.

"You don't have to ask my permission to come in here, Rachel."

"I don't want to impose on you."

"You are not imposing if you are supposed to be here."

"Well I don't want you to think that I'm trying to make you do something that you don't want." Rachel sat in a chair across from Birdie.

Birdie wondered why they couldn't have a conversation without sparring with each other. "It's a little late for that, isn't it?"

"What does that mean?"

"That means that this afternoon when you told Rosa to go with Little Rachel and me to go with you I wasn't given a choice, was I?"

"I asked you what you wanted, didn't I?"

"It was more like you told me."

"Well I'm sorry," Rachel snorted. "I had other things on my mind and I needed to take care of them."

"Rachel, you don't think anyone else is capable of doing things for themselves."

"No, I don't."

"Yes, you do." Birdie stood up almost knocking over her chair.

Rachel stood up. "I'm not in the mood right now to argue with you Birdie. I have a lot of things on my mind."

"We all do, Rachel, we...."

"I signed the ranch over to Mathews."

"What?"

"That's where I've been." Rachel took the paper out of her shirt pocket. "I can't make payment to Mathews any other way so I signed the ranch over to him."

Birdie read the paper. "Are you sure this is what you want?"

"I don't know of any other way. It has the lien and the quarantine and he is an attorney so he can figure out what to do with it if I go to jail."

"Rachel, you aren't going to jail, so don't say that."

"I need to make sure that you and everyone else are taken care of." Rachel sat back down. "I told him that if I go to jail then you would be the foreman. If I don't go to jail then I will be."

"What did he say?"

"He refused to sign it. I told him that if he didn't sign it then I would go to court without him."

"Rachel, you are so hard headed some times."

"I am not."

"Yes, you are." Birdie shook her head. "It's got to be your way or nothing else."

"I don't know how else to be," Rachel snapped back at her. "It's helped me keep the ranch going despite everything that's been going on."

Birdie could see the pain and worry in Rachel's eyes and didn't want to argue with her. She knew Rachel believed herself to be a failure when she signed the ranch over to Mathews. "Let's not talk about that."

"Why not? It's a very real possibility."

"That's why you hired Mathews, isn't it?"

"Yeah, I guess."

"Sometimes, Rachel, you have to let other people help you. It's not a sign of weakness."

"It's hard to do that."

"Think of it as another way protecting yourself and the ranch."

"I guess if you put it that way it makes sense," Rachel

sighed. "I know that I can be demanding and hard to convince to change my ways, but it's been so hard, Birdie. It used to be so easy for me when we were together. You were the one I leaned on when things didn't go right. I didn't really understand how much I loved and needed you until you were gone. When you didn't come back I gave up. I had no reason to believe I could ever love that way again. I believed I had to be hard hearted to survive. I took no quarter and gave none—not until you came back into my life. I ain't going to say I will change over night but with your help I can say that I will do my best."

"It's been a long journey for both of us, Rachel. It's not going to be easy and will take some time but we can do it." Birdie put her hand on Rachel's shoulder. "It's getting late and we will be up early tomorrow. It's time we turned in for the night."

"Okay." Rachel walked to the door. "Let me know when you are ready for bed and I'll come back in."

"No, don't go."

"I need to do it this way, Birdie. If I don't I may do something that would jeopardize us. I've worked too hard to gain your trust and in the mood I'm in right now I'd be an ass and lose it."

Birdie kissed Rachel's cheek then kissed her on the lips. Rachel grabbed Birdie's arms and held them behind her back as she returned the kiss. She forced her tongue into her mouth when Birdie tried to push herself away. She gripped the back of Birdie's blouse, trying to rip it off. Birdie struggled to get her arms free. Rachel knew if she didn't leave the room that she wouldn't stop. She pushed Birdie away from her. "I've got to get out of here."

"It's okay, Rachel." Birdie grabbed her arm. "If that's the way you want us to be together its okay."

"No Birdie, not this way." Rachel held up her hands. "I want you too much right now, Birdie." She opened the door and left.

Rachel sat in the lobby of the hotel watching the lamp

lighter turn on the gas globes. She thought about what she did to Birdie and wondered why in the hell acted the way she did. She had been so careful all the times they were together on the ranch. She was waiting for the right time to get close then when the opportunity came about she screwed it up. She leaned back in the chair and looked at the ceiling. Why couldn't I just leave it alone, she said aloud as she ran her hand through her hair? She saved Birdie from the men in the alley only to discover that with little provocation she was just like them.

She walked up the stairs to the room hoping Birdie was already asleep. Slowly turning the door knob, she peeked around the door. The light of the gas lamp outside the window was bright enough for her to see Birdie lying nude on the bed. She remembered Birdie never liked to go to bed with any clothes on. She thought about the hot springs and how soft Birdie's skin was when they lay next to each other. She wanted more than anything to touch Birdie and show her how much she loved her. Standing next to the bed she knew this would be harder than she thought it would be. Good night my love, she whispered as she pulled the blanket up over Birdie's shoulders. She lay down on the bed and stared at the ceiling. Her heart was pounding, and it was all she could do not to reach over and touch Birdie. She turned away from Birdie thinking that she couldn't be like the rest of them. No matter what she felt she wouldn't be like the rest of them.

Chapter Thirty-seven

Mathews stood on the top step of the courthouse looking at the crowd that had gathered to hear the case. He wondered which ones wanted Rachel to be convicted so they could start proceedings to get the ranch. What would they think if they found out that Rachel had signed it over to him? He knew most of them had come for the entertainment of it all. That was usually what happened when there was to be a hanging. Day after day and year after year the ranchers and farmers did the same thing over and over, and when something like a hanging was to take place it was a reason to get together with old friends. The hotels and boarding houses filled up with families taking time off from their back breaking work to see the spectacle. Families camped out on the lawn in the town square to get a good spot to see it all. This wasn't going to be a hanging, but it did involve one of their own and it could have a devastating effect on the largest ranch in the valley. The crowd grew silent as Rachel and the others walked past them to the door.

"It's good to see you," Mathews said.

"Yeah, I guess." Rachel looked back at the crowd. "One would think that there's going to be a hanging."

"Not today or any other day if I have my way." Mathews put his hand on her shoulder. "Let's get inside."

Not a chair in the gallery was empty. People were standing along the back wall and out the door. Rachel sat next to Mathews in front of the railing that separated the courtroom. Birdie, Little Rachel, and Rosa sat in the chairs behind them. To their left was the lawyer for the court. Rachel looked at the men sitting behind him trying to remember who was in the alley.

"All rise and come to order. This court is now in session," The bailiff standing in the front of the room said. "The honorable Judge Macaffey is presiding."

The judge walked through a side door and stepped onto the bench. He took a watch out of his vest and looked at it. They all stood and waited until the he sat down behind the bench.

"You may be seated," the judge said, looking around the courtroom. "Good morning to all who have come here. Mr. Crossley and Mr. Mathews, I hope the two of you are ready for I do not suffer lightly when a proceeding takes place and one is not prepared. Mr. Crossley, are you ready?"

"Yes sir, I am." Crossley stood up.

"Good. Mr. Mathews, are you ready?"

Mathews stood up. "Yes, I am, your honor."

"Mr. Crossley, what say you about this matter before this court?"

"Your honor I am here to prosecute the defendant, Rachel O'Callahan for willfully and deliberately shooting a Mr. Hadley Corchoran on June nineteenth of this year in the town of Yerington. The defendant did use a shotgun in the course of the shooting, and Mr. Corchoran is very lucky to have survived. I intend to see that Miss O'Callahan is found guilty of this heinous crime. Thank you, your honor."

"Thank you, Mr. Crossley." The judge leaned back in his chair. "Mr. Mathews, what say you?"

"Thank you, your honor. I will show the court that Rachel O'Callahan did what any law abiding citizen would do to protect the life of another person. Thank you."

The judge scratched his beard. "Well allrighty then. Mr. Crossley, you can start."

"Thank you, your honor. I would like to start by calling Mr. Hadley Corchoran to the stand."

Rachel watched Hadley Corchoran walk to the chair to be sworn in. She listened to the bailiff as he asked about the truth, the whole truth, and nothing but the truth, thinking about what happened in the alley. He sat down in the chair.

"Mr. Corchoran, I thank you for coming all the way here from Stockton, California to attend this court."

Corchoran smiled and waved his hand at the lawyer. "It's only fitting that I come here to see that she gets what's coming to her."

The judge leaned over the desk. "Mr. Corchoran, please do not speak your mind unless you are asked."

"Uh, yes sir."

"Mr. Crossley, you may continue."

"Thank you, your honor." Crossley walked up to the rail in front of the chair. "Mr. Corcoran, please tell the court what happened on the night of June nineteenth of this year."

"Me and my brother," he pointed at Bailey sitting behind Crossley's desk, "me and him were on our way to Stockton to work for a new outfit and stopped in town for a little while. We got some grub and decided to find a saloon and maybe a woman or two. We found a saloon and had a few then decided to go on ahead to Stockton. When we left the saloon a Indian woman offered herself to us so we took her up on it."

"What do you mean when you say that she offered her favors?" Crossley asked.

"You know," Corchoran shrugged his shoulders, "things that men like."

"Did you and your brother partake of these favors?"

"Well, uh yeah. I mean I was trying to. My brother didn't have a chance to do anything."

"You didn't get to finish?" Crossley asked.

"She took us into that alley and told us she would give us what we wanted for a couple of dollars. I tried to get my money's worth, but the next thing I knew that woman over there shot me." He pointed at Rachel.

"Are you sure that is the woman who shot you?"

"Sure as I am sitting here."

"Why did she shoot you?" Crossley pointed at Rachel.

"I don't know. I got off that Indian woman like she asked me to then the next thing I know she shoots me."

"Mr. Corchoran, I know that this is a very embarrassing question, but I must ask you to tell the court where she shot you."

"In that alley," Corchoran said. He could hear people talking and giggling.

"I meant where on your body did she shoot you?"

In a voice barely above a whisper he said, "Between my legs."

The judge leaned across the bench. "Please speak up so everyone can hear you."

"Between my legs." Corchoran put his hands on his lap to keep everyone from looking at his crotch.

"Quiet." The judge started banging with the gavel. "I'll not have any laughing about this matter in this courtroom."

Crossley waited until it was quiet before questioning Corchoran again. "Did you provoke her?"

"No."

"You did nothing at all to provoke her?"

"No sir. I couldn't as I was on top of that Indian woman and all. She made me get off the Indian woman, and when I tried to pull my breeches up she wouldn't let me. I told her it wasn't decent to be like that then she shot me."

"Mr. Corchoran, what type of fire arm did she use?"

"A shotgun."

"Are you sure it was a shotgun?"

Corchoran leaned over the rail in front if his chair. "I'ffin you were shot where I was you'd sure as hell remember what type of gun it was, wouldn't you?"

Crossley didn't answer.

"I said wouldn't you?"

"Quiet." The judge hit the gavel to stop the laughter. "I said quiet."

"It was the one over there." He pointed at the shotgun on the table in front of Rachel.

"Mr. Corchoran, do you have children?"

"No."

"Did you plan on having children?"

"Yeah, me and my woman were gonna have a passel of 'em."

Crossley walked to the table where Rachel sat and looked at her. "Mr. Corchoran, will you be able to have children now?"

"Hell no...thanks to that bitch." Corchoran stood up and pointed at Rachel.

The judge slammed the gavel on the desk. "Mr. Corchoran, I'll have none of that language in the court room. Do you hear me?"

"Yes sir." He sat down.

"Mr. Crossley, I expect you to keep your client in line."

"Yes, your honor." Crossley cleared his throat. "Mr. Corchoran, your brother took you to the doctor, didn't he?"

"Yep, he put me on the saddle and took me to the doc."

"Did she help you at all?"

"Nope. She just stood there and watched."

"Your honor, I would like to excuse this witness."

The judge nodded his head.

"Mr. Corchoran, you may go back to your seat."

Crossley waited until Corchoran sat down.

"Your honor I would like to say that it is a sad thing that my client won't ever be able to experience the joy of fatherhood because of the heinous crime put upon him by the defendant."

"Mr. Crossley, you may address that when all the testimony is through. Call your next witness."

"I call Bailey Corchoran to the stand."

Bailey sat down after being sworn in.

"Mr. Corchoran, you were in the alley the same time as your brother at the time this crime occurred?"

"Yep."

Mason Valley Ranch

"Tell us what happened that night, in your words."

"Like Hadley said, we was going to Stockton when we stopped to get some grub and rest. We walked past that alley and a Indian woman offered herself up to us so Hadley took her first. He was on top of her when a woman with a gun came into the alley and put the gun to Hadley's head. She told him to get off the Indian woman and when he did she shot him."

"Did your brother in any way provoke her to shoot him?"

Bailey scratched his beard and looked at the ceiling. "Naw, I cain't say he did."

Crossley leaned against the rail. "If you were in the alley with them why didn't you help your brother?"

"I was watching that big black dog of hers. He wasn't but two or three feet away from me, and I didn't want to get dog bit."

"Did she threaten you also?"

"After she shot Hadley she did ask me if I had any business with her. I told her that I didn't think so and she told me to get him to the doctor."

"Did she offer to help you?"

"Naw, she just told me to get the horses and get him on out of there. I didn't want to get like Hadley so I did skedaddled and did what she told me to."

"Thank you Mr. Corchoran, I think that is all."

"Your honor that is all that I have at this time," Crossley said.

"Are you sure?" the judge asked.

"Yes." Crossley sat in his chair.

"Mr. Mathews, are you ready for your rebuttal now?"

"Yes, sir." Mathews stood up. "I would like to call Bailey Corchoran back to the stand."

"You are still under oath," the judge said to Bailey as he sat down in the chair.

"Mr. Corchoran, you said that the Indian woman offered herself up to you, did you not?"

"Yep."

"You said that she led you into the alley."

"Yep."

"If she did, then why did you and your brother have the rope?"

"Huh?" Bailey had a puzzled look on his face.

"Why did you and your brother tie the Indian woman's hands up then tie them to a post? Was it so your brother could have his way with her?"

Bailey squirmed in the chair.

"Did the Indian woman fight with you and your brother?"

"Uh yeah...but sometimes they like it like that."

"That Indian woman didn't offer herself to you and your brother, did she?" Mathews leaned over the rail.

Bailey wiped his mouth with his hand.

"You and your brother forced that Indian woman into that alley, didn't you?"

Bailey looked at his brother for an answer.

"Mr. Corchoran, you are under oath."

"Maybe...I guess."

"Did you or did you not force that Indian woman into that alley for the pleasure of you and your brother?"

"Yeah."

"You tied her up so he could take advantage of her, and then you sat on that crate waiting for your turn at her, didn't you?"

"Yeah."

"You saw the shooting, didn't you?"

"Yeah."

Mathews walked to the table and picked up Rachel's shotgun. He opened the breech to look down the barrels then snapped it shut and put it back on the table. "Did Miss O'Callahan fight with your brother?"

"She didn't fight fists with him, if that's what you mean," Bailey said.

"Did she provoke him in any way?"

"Naw." He put his fingers on his lips then his eyes widened. "She got real mad at him though."

"What makes you say that?"

"They was talking about him leaving that Indian woman alone when he said something that got her right upset."

"What did he say?"

"He told her," Bailey ran his hands through his hair, "he told her that it was nothing but an Indian bitch anyway. She got a real crazy look in her eyes and put that shotgun between his legs. Next thing I know he was rolling all over the ground bellowing about how she shot his balls off."

The judge banged on the gavel to stop the laughing. "None of that or I'll have everyone removed from here." He leaned towards Bailey. "Mr. Corchoran, we will refer to them as testicles."

"What?" Bailey looked at the judge.

"For the court's sake we will call them testicles."

"Uh huh." Bailey shook his head.

"Go on, Mr. Corchoran." The judge sat back in his chair.

"What happened then?" Mathews asked.

"She walked over to me and asked if I had any business with the Indian woman or her and I said that I reckon that I did not. She told me I should get my brother and myself out of there. I told her I didn't think he could ride at that particular moment, and she pointed the gun at me and said that if I didn't get him out of her sight then I might not be riding too well either."

"Have you and your brother had problems like this before?" Mathews picked up a piece of paper from the table.

"Naw, I cain't recollect so."

"What about Kansas City?"

He adjusted himself in the chair. "Kansas City?"

"Isn't it because of your brother you two are working out west in Stockton? Your brother and his eye for the women?"

Bailey grinned. "He does get along pretty good with the women I guess."

"By getting along, do you mean how he forces himself on the women?"

"No not all of the time. Sometimes he gets along with

them pretty good."

"Sometimes meaning not in Kansas City or Denver or Cheyenne?" Mathews put the paper on the rail in front of Bailey. "Do you know what this is Mr. Corchoran?"

Bailey leaned over to look at the paper. "No sir, cause I cain't read too well."

"It is a summons for Hadley Corchoran and you, Bailey. This one is from Kansas City, and on the table I have a couple more from Denver and Cheyenne. Tell us, Mr. Corchoran, why do you and your brother move around so much?"

Bailey looked at his brother and shrugged his shoulders. "Hadley has some people looking for him right now."

"Who?" Mathews asked.

"Women...and the law I guess." Bailey sat back in the chair.

"Isn't one of them his wife back in Tennessee?" Mathews held up another piece of paper.

"Yeah."

"What does she want with him?"

Bailey wiped his face with his hands. "She caught him with one of her sisters and chased him out of the house with a knife. He came and got me and we left."

"How many children does your brother have?"

"Let's see I reckon eight or nine...no wait," he counted on his fingers while he talked, "there's some...there's one or two papooses up in Wyoming I think."

"How many women have had his children?"

"I don't rightly know."

"You'd like to go back to Tennessee, wouldn't you, Mr. Corchoran?"

"Yep."

"But you can't, can you?"

"Nope."

"Why can't you?" Mathews crossed his arms while Bailey talked.

"Me and him is real close. He don't think too proper sometimes and I worry about that. I try to keep him out of trouble as much as I can, but it gets real hard."

"Could you explain that?"

He scratched his head. "I keep telling him he's just gotta keep his pants up. I want to go back home, but we gotta stay out here for a spell yet. That is until Sissy, his wife back in Tennessee, calms down. Back home when a woman gets riled up you can hide out in the woods for a time then go back home when it all blows over. Out here if you get a woman riled up they get Johnny law after you. The women out here carry guns and pistols and they can shoot real good. I want to go home because there's no place to hide out here. Hell, a man goes to do his business out in the sage brush and everyone in the next county can see him. When we left that saloon and he saw that Indian woman I told him to leave her be. I told him that one day he would get his b..." He looked at the judge. "What did you call them?"

The judge leaned over the bench. "Testicles."

Bailey looked at the ceiling silently mouthing the word then shook his head. "Testicles. I told him that one of them women or a jealous husband would flat shoot them off if he didn't watch it. Well, it finally happened."

"That will be all, Mr. Corchoran." Mathews sat in his chair.

"Mr. Crossley, is there anything else you need of him?" the judge asked.

Crossley shook his head.

"Mr. Crossley, is there anything else to present to the court?"

"Ah...yes, your honor. I would like to call Miss Rachel O'Callahan to the stand now."

Mathews put his hand on Rachel's arm. "Just remember to answer only what he asks and don't elaborate on anything."

The bailiff swore her in then told her to sit down. Crossley walked up to the rail and put his hand on it.

"Miss O'Callahan, you have admitted to shooting Mr. Corchoran?"

"Yes."

"Might I ask why?"

"Why what?" Rachel answered.

Crossley folded his arms. "Don't get smart with me, Miss O'Callahan."

Rachel folded her arms. "You asked a question, and I answered it."

"Judge."

"Yes Mr. Crossley?" The judge said.

"Tell this witness that she must answer my questions."

"She did answer it." He looked at Rachel. "It would help this court a great deal later not to be so concise in your answers, Miss O'Callahan."

"Yes sir, your honor."

Crossley paced in front of her. "Why did you shoot Hadley Corchoran, who was unarmed in that alley?"

"He was taking advantage of a woman and she couldn't defend herself."

"You knew that for a fact?"

"Not until I walked into that alley."

"You were looking for a fight with someone, anyone, that night, weren't you?"

"No."

"You have been quite upset for quite a spell now, haven't you?" He propped his hands on the railing.

"About what?" Rachel answered.

"Isn't it true that your ranch has a lien on it and your cattle have been quarantined?"

"Yes." Rachel wondered what that had to do with the shooting.

"You took all of your frustration and being mad out on that cowboy in that alley didn't you?"

"No!"

"Truth is that you just wanted to avenge some of the things that are going on and you saw those cowboys and you shot them for spite of everything."

Mathews jumped up. "Your honor, I see no reasoning for this questioning of Miss O'Callahan. This has no bearing on what happened in that alley."

"Your honor." Crossley held up his arms. "I am simply trying to find out why a seemingly sane and rational woman would be in an alley that time of night shooting an unarmed man."

The judge looked at Mathews and Crossley. "Miss O'Callahan, answer the question."

"It is true that there is a lien on the ranch," Rachel snapped back at him. "I still own it, and I don't plan to lose it to anyone for no reason"

"You've been under the lien for quite a spell now, haven't you?"

"Yes." She wrapped her hands around the ends of the chair because she wanted to get out of the chair and punch Crossley in the mouth.

"Would you say that it has skewed your way of thinking about things lately?"

"No," Rachel snapped back at him.

"When you saw those men in that alley you thought you could take your frustration out on them, isn't that right, Miss O'Callahan?"

"No."

"What did you mean to do to those men in that alley?" Crossley leaned over the rail.

Rachel leaned forward. "I meant to do what I did."

"To kill them?"

She pointed at Hadley and Bailey. "To get them away from her."

"Did she ask for your help?"

"She couldn't."

"How did you know? Did you ask her?"

"No."

"Then how did you know? Is it because she may not have wanted you to interfere?"

Rachel massaged the arm of the chair with her hand. "It was because I saw him," she pointed at Bailey, "knock her to the ground and bind her hands together, then he tied her hands to a post. By the time I got into the alley his brother was already having his way with her."

"So instead of getting the sheriff you took things into your own hands." He sat down in the chair behind his table. "I have no more questions for her, your honor."

"Mr. Mathews, you may start," the judge said.

He walked around the table. "Miss O'Callahan, why did you go into that alley you're your shotgun?"

"I saw two men beating up on a woman, and I wanted to stop them."

"Did you have to take the shotgun?"

"There were two men," she said.

"Why did you shoot him?" Mathews pointed at Hadley. "Did he try to attack you?"

"No. It was...what he...uh...said about her." Rachel looked down at her hands.

"And what did he say?"

"That she was just a Indian bitch."

"Did you know who the woman was?"

"I recognized who she was after I got into the alley."

"Who was it?"

Rachel didn't answer.

"Rachel, you must tell us who it was in the alley," Mathews said.

Rachel shook her head no.

The judge looked at her. "Miss O'Callahan, it will be to your benefit to answer all the questions."

The sheriff walked through the door of the court room. "Your honor, may I please speak to you?"

The judge waved him up to the bench. After a brief conference the judge told everyone to be back in court in three hours and banged the gavel on the bench top. Mathews walked up to the rail. "You are doing fine."

Rachel covered her face with her hands. "It won't be long now before you get yourself a cattle ranch, Mr. Mathews."

"The fight isn't over. Why don't all of you go on back to the hotel and rest? I'll meet you back here."

"Okay."

Birdie, Little Rachel, and Rosa followed her out of the courthouse.

"You go on, and I'll join you in a while," Birdie said. "There's something I need to do."

She walked away before Rachel or Rosa could say anything to her. Two hours later she walked into the room at the hotel.

"I was worried about you," Rachel said.

"I'm fine," Birdie said as she sat in the chair.

Rachel wondered where Birdie had been, but it was clear she wasn't in the mood to talk so nothing more was said.

Chapter Thirty-eight

Major Wilson looked at himself in the mirror behind the bar then drank a shot of whiskey from the bottle the bartender had given him. He wasn't in too bad of shape after more than twenty years out in the western desert. His hair was a little gray at the temples, but that was an advantage with the ladies. He didn't have the big gut most men his age had. That was useful when taking care of the ladies in bed. He was eastern born and bred and followed his father to West Point. He tried to get a position in the Lincoln cabinet, but he was assigned out in the field. It wasn't his fault he couldn't get the lead in the choice battles because of the inferior commanders above him. At the end of the war he was given a choice to retire and get a job at his uncle's furniture shop or go west to command a fort. The fort wasn't what he expected, but it was better than scraping wood and smelling glue all day. He raised the glass and gave himself a silent salute in the mirror. He swallowed the liquid and pulled a piece of paper from his shirt pocket. He had planned on being at Rachel O'Callahan's trial anyway, but he had a summons from the sheriff to attend.

"Sergeant, the trial will wind up this afternoon and after the sentencing of that bitch tomorrow you and I will ride out to my ranch. I've got the papers signed, and all I need to do is get them over to the county recorder's office for validation.

Mason Valley Ranch

I've waited a long time to get my hands on that property, and it is even sweeter the way I am going to get it. I can't believe the bitch made it so easy for me." He poured another drink for himself and one for the sergeant. "Let's get on over there and see the show."

"Major Wilson, what brings you here?" Big Jake walked up the steps behind the major.

"I came to see the show. I've had my eye on a piece of property, and after this trial I can finally put my retirement papers in and be the gentleman rancher."

"It wouldn't be that big spread to the southwest of the valley I keep hearing about, would it?" Big Jake propped his arms on the barrel of his rifle. "I'd watch myself if I were you. From the talk I hear around town there's a lot of interest in that ranch."

The major took some papers from his pocket and waved them in the air. "There can be all the interest anyone wants, but I've got the papers and it will be mine in a few hours."

"When is the proceeding going to start?" Big Jake asked.

The major looked at his pocketwatch and snapped the top shut. "In a little while. The judge recessed for a few hours because the sheriff had to talk to him. What are you doing here?"

"I am passing through going down to Arizona. I heard about the trial and thought I'd see what was going on. I'm heading on in to get a seat."

"Excuse me, gentlemen," Mathews said as he and Rachel walked past the major and the sergeant.

"I see you've gotten yourself into a hornet's nest, Rachel," the major said. "You should have taken me up on my proposals. You be sure and come see me after the trial and we can talk about what's going to happen to the ranch. That is subject to the outcome of course. I'll be waiting out here to talk when, or might I say if, you come back."

Mathews put his hand on Rachel's arm to keep her from hitting the major. "Come Rachel, let's get inside."

The major said sneered at her. "A man wouldn't have put

the ranch in jeopardy."

Mathews gripped harder on her arm and forced her inside the courthouse. "Rachel, he's trying to get you riled up to help the prosecution's case. Sit down and don't think about that right now."

Rachel knew Mathews was right. She sat down and faced the front of the courtroom, knowing that if she looked back to see the major she would start a fight and it wouldn't help at all. Through it all she had fought back against the lien and the quarantine and the fire. She knew that the ranch would be a prize for anyone, but she was the owner and she wasn't about to lose it. She had grown up in the valley and knew most everyone there. She knew they had come to see the trial not caring if she was guilty or not but to be social and see friends they wouldn't ordinarily see. She did find it curious though that Mathews was the only one that really believed she was innocent of the charges. She felt a hand on her shoulder and looked around to see Rosa and Rachel sit down.

"Where is Birdie?" she asked Rosa.

"She say to go on ahead to courthouse. She will be along soon."

"All rise. The court is now in session."

The judge sat in his chair and hit the gavel on the bench. "We will now proceed with the case. Miss O'Callahan, you may come back up here, and remember, you are still under oath."

"Yes sir," Rachel said as she sat down.

"Mr. Mathews, you can continue with you're questioning of the defendant."

"Miss O'Callahan, you stated earlier that you went into an alley to help protect a woman in dire need."

"Yes, I did."

"Did you know who was in that alley when you first went in there?"

"No."

"So it was just two men accosting a woman."

"Yes."

"Did you finally recognize the woman?"

"Yes."

"Who was the woman?"

Rachel didn't want to tell them Birdie's name. She looked at the chair where Birdie should have been.

"Miss O'Callahan, I must ask again for you to tell us who was in that alley."

"What does it matter?" Rachel answered.

"You must answer the question," the judge said.

"It was a friend of mine."

"Who?"

"It was Birdie Perez."

"How long have you known this friend?"

"We grew up together on the ranch until...."

"Until what?"

Rachel looked at the major as she spoke. "Until the cavalry came and took her and her family away."

"Would you have gone into that alley if it had not been your friend?"

"Yeah."

Mathews picked up the shotgun and held it above his head. "Would you have taken the shotgun?"

"Yes."

"Did you intend to kill those men?"

"No."

"Then why did you go into that alley with that shotgun?"

"I wanted to get them away from her and bring her home where she belongs...with me."

"I think that will be all, Miss O'Callahan."

"Do you have any questions of her, Mr. Crossley?" the judge asked.

"No, your honor."

"You may step down, Miss O'Callahan. Is there anyone else either one of you would like to call at this time?"

"No," Crossley said

"Yes, your honor," Mathews said. "I have one more witness to present."

"Then please do, Mr. Mathews."

"Your honor, may I please talk to my client for a moment?" Mathews asked.

"Just for a few moments."

Mathews leaned over the table to talk to Rachel. "I want you to promise me that no matter what happens you will not leave from behind this table."

"I don't understand," Rachel said.

"I need a promise, Rachel. You have to trust me now, and I need your promise not to leave this table no matter what happens."

Rachel wondered what the attorney was up to. "You have my promise."

"Okay." He stood midway between the table and the judge's bench. "Your honor I would like to call Birdie Perez to the stand."

"No." Rachel jumped up, knocking her chair over.

"Sit down, Miss O'Callahan." The judge hit the gavel on the desk. "I do not want any more of that in this court."

The bailiff picked up her chair and motioned for her to sit down.

Mathews motioned to the deputy standing by the door to open it. Birdie walked into the courtroom.

Rachel stood up again. "I don't want her to testify."

"Mr. Mathews, please restrain your client before she is in contempt of this court."

"Rachel, please sit down. This is what she wanted."

Birdie looked straight ahead at the judge as she walked between the chairs in the gallery. At the third row of seats Big Jake stood up and yelled.

"She can't testify."

"Why not?" the judge asked

"She's mine."

"What in tarnation are you talking about?" the judge asked.

"I paid good money for her a few years back. She's still

got work to do for me to pay her debt."

"Who are you, and what are you talking about?"

He walked to the end of the row. "I'm Big Jake. I bought her fair and square." He took a piece of paper out of a pouch and waved it in the air. "She cost me good money."

"Bailiff, bring that piece of paper to me."

The judge read the paper and lay it down on the bench. "Sheriff Griffey, join me in my chambers?"

The sheriff followed the judge into the adjoining room. Mathews looked at Rachel and shrugged his shoulders. The judge returned to the bench. He pointed at Big Jake. "You will sit down and say nothing else while this trial is proceeding. Do you hear me?

"You're mine," Big Jake said to Birdie before he sat down.

"Mr. Mathews, you can continue."

"Thank you, your honor." Mathews took Birdie's hand and led her to the front of the courtroom. "Bailiff, you can swear her in now."

Crossley stood up. "He can't do that, your honor. She is an Indian, and Indians can't swear on the bible."

"I will be the judge of that, Mr. Crossley. I think this woman has a great bearing on this case so I will allow her to speak."

"Her testimony won't be valid because she is an Indian," Crossley said.

The judge was getting irritated. "Bailiff, swear this woman in."

Birdie placed her hand on the bible and looked at Rachel as she answered the bailiff.

"Do you understand what you are about to do here?" the judge asked her.

"Yes your honor, I do."

"I will not tolerate any more outbursts from anyone. Mr. Mathews, you may continue."

"Miss Perez, please tell the court about that night in the alley."

"I was walking past the old grist mill when a man grabbed me and pulled me into the alley."

"Why were you down there?"

"I was going home."

"From where?"

"Sadie J's Saloon."

"Why were you in that establishment?"

"I...I worked there to keep the men from being lonely." She looked down at the floor.

"Did you see these two men in that saloon?"

"No."

"Did you offer the men anything before you were accosted?"

"No. I had never seen them before."

Crossley stood up. "Your honor, I see no reason to continue with this questioning. This woman is only befouling the good name of these two men."

"Mr. Crossley, sit down. Mr. Mathews, continue on."

"Do you think you would be here today if it weren't for Miss O'Callahan coming into that alley?"

"No."

"Miss Perez, I must ask you some things that won't be nice, but I need you to answer so I can help Miss O'Callahan. Do you understand me?"

"Yes, I do." She looked at Rachel.

"Your honor, I must ask some questions of this witness that may seem a bit odd, but I must ask that you please bear with me for a while. I am sure that having read that piece of paper you should understand why I will ask the questions. In a little while it should be clear why my client did what she did."

"Your honor, this Indian is not on trial here." Crossley pointed at Rachel. "That woman over there is."

"Mr. Crossley, sit down and shut up. Mr. Mathews, I will let you ask questions, but be careful."

"Thank you, your honor." Mathews stood in front of Birdie. "Miss Perez, were you taken from your home by the cavalry?"

"Yes."

"Were you taken to the Pyramid Reservation?"

"No. We were taken across the mountains then sold to Big Jake."

"Mr. Mathews." The judge held up his hand to stop the questioning. "Miss Perez, if I hear you right you said that you were sold."

"Yes."

"As if someone would sell cattle?"

"Yes."

The judge looked at Big Jake then leaned back in his chair. "You can continue, Mr. Mathews."

"You said 'we,' Miss Perez. How many other women were with you?"

"Twenty."

"Were all the women sold?"

"No." Birdie bit her lower lip to keep from crying. "Some were traded back for me. Big Jake didn't have enough money for them and me so he left them behind."

"That's a lie." Big Jake jumped up from his chair.

"Sit down or I'll have you taken into custody," the judge said. "Bailiff, the next time he says something, put him in jail."

"Major, are you going to sit there and let her say those things?" Big Jake looked at Major Wilson.

"I don't know what you're talking about," the major said.

"Both of you be quiet," the judge said. "Mr. Mathews, continue."

"What happened to those women left behind?"

"They shot them."

"Who shot them?"

Birdie did not know that Major Wilson was in the room until Big Jake talked to him. She also saw Sergeant Crouse sitting next to him. She wanted to testify, but she knew they could arrest her.

"Miss Perez," Mathews asked again. "Who shot them?"

The judge leaned forward. "You must answer the question."

"The soldiers."

"Are you telling us that U.S. Cavalry soldiers shot those

women, Miss Perez?"

Birdie nodded her head.

"What happened after that?" Mathews asked.

"I...we were taken west to the gold camps and made to please the miners."

"What if you didn't do as you were told?"

"We were beaten."

"Your honor, I must really object to this sham of a defense. This is an admitted woman of low character, and to sit here and listen to this is pure dribble."

"Mr. Crossley, I said shut up. One more time and you're out of this courtroom."

Crossley threw his hands up in the air and sat down in his chair.

"When did you last see Big Jake?"

"He left me beside the Klamath River to die. I had been wounded after fighting with Frenchy, his captain. A quaker woman and her son found me and took me to the mission they had near Fort Klamath. They took care of me until I could go home."

"What happened then?"

"A bounty hunter captured me and took me to a camp up in Montana. The camp was attacked by a band of Nez Perce, and after the fighting was over I went with them to Canada."

"Why would you go with them and not come home?"

"I couldn't come home because I am an Indian. I would be put on the reservation and not be able to live where I was born."

"Your honor, I do not understand what this has to do with anything about this case," Crossley said.

"Mr. Mathews, would you like to explain?"

"Not at this time, your honor, but please let me continue as all will be able to understand in a little while."

"Make it a short while, Mr. Mathews," the judge said.

Mathews shook his head. "Do you have a child, Miss Perez?

"Yes. I married a Swedish man and had a baby girl. We

lived up near the Canadian border where he had a mining claim. He was bushwhacked for the claim, but he had put the claim in the baby's name. They took my baby away from me and gave her to a white man and his wife. After they adopted her and took control of the mining claim, they left her on a reservation in Montana."

"What did you do after that?"

"I started working in saloons and tending to the wants of the patrons." Birdie looked at Rachel. "I had nothing to live for."

"Thank you, Miss Perez, that is all," Mathews said.

Birdie stepped down from the witness box. Mathews put his hand on her arm to stop her. "Please forgive me." He grabbed her blouse ripping the buttons off and pulled it down over her shoulders.

"No," Rachel shouted and jumped up.

"Remember your promise." Mathews pointed at her.

Crossley jumped up. "Your honor, what in the hell is going on here?

The judge beat on the gavel to quiet the room. "Mr. Mathews, have you lost your mind completely? Cover this woman up.

"No, your honor, I haven't lost my mind. I need to show this court why my client would be of the mind to do something like she did and this is why."

Birdie turned to face the judge.

"This woman is the life long friend of my client. She was taken from her home here in this valley and subjected to a life no one should have to live. She has been raped, beaten, and scarred beyond what anyone should have to endure. I'm sure when my client went into that alley and realized it was her friend and saw what she had been subjected to all she cared about was saving her life." Mathews took his jacket off and wrapped it around Birdie's shoulders. "Your honor, you are a learned man and I hope you will understand the context of what I am going to say now. As you know, women are subjected to laws made by men and governed by men. They can't have real property unless it comes from parental inheritance. If they marry and something happens to the husband then the property can be taken by any male of the husband's family as his own, even though it was hers by inheritance. The woman must abide by the laws. If the man who inherits the property decides he doesn't want the woman there he can evict her. Women who are relieved of their property must try and make a life however they can. Sometimes they will find another husband. Sometimes they eke out an existence as best they can. Sometimes they will find another woman to live with and pool their resources. Back east when two women live together to make ends meet or for convenience it is known as a Boston Marriage. What ever the reason they are together it should be clear to the court that there is a bond between my client and Miss Perez." He pointed at Rachel. "I just hope that if I ever need a friend that it would be someone like my client."

"I think this court has seen enough for today. I will consider all of the testimony and give my decision tomorrow. Court will reconvene tomorrow at nine o'clock in the morning." The judge hit the gavel and walked out of the room.

Mathews escorted Birdie back to the table.

"Why Birdie?" Rachel asked. "You didn't have to do that."

"I can't live on that ranch without you."

"Why don't you go on back to the hotel? We won't know anything before tomorrow anyway," Mathews said.

No one said anything on the walk back to the hotel. Rosa took Little Rachel up to their room while Rachel and Birdie stayed in the lobby.

Birdie sat down on a chair. "What do you think will happen?"

"I wish I knew, Birdie." Rachel sat next to her. "Things are so out of hand right now that I don't want to think about it."

A man with a newspaper stood in front of Birdie and cleared his throat. Birdie looked at him but didn't move.

"I want that chair," he said to her.

"Mister," Rachel picked up the shotgun, "if she has to

move then you won't be sitting down anytime too soon yourself."

"I'll get the desk clerk and we'll see who moves," the man said.

The desk clerk picked up a newspaper to show the man the front page. "That's them."

The man read the article about the trial. "Oh my gosh."

Rachel watched him walk out of the hotel and set the shotgun on the floor next to the chair.

Chapter Thirty-nine

Standing at the doorway of the courthouse the following morning was Major Wilson. Birdie stopped when she saw him.

"What's the matter?" Rachel asked.

"It's him. He's the one that sold me to Big Jake."

"Are you sure?"

"Yes, I'm positive."

"Is there a problem?" Mathews asked as he walked up behind them.

"Birdie says that Major Wilson is the one that sold her to Big Jake."

"He can't do anything now."

"Come on, Birdie, I'm right beside you." Rachel took her arm as they walked up the steps.

The major stopped talking to the men with whom he was standing and tipped his hat to them. "I'll be waiting here after the trial."

"Go to hell," Rachel said when she opened the door.

The people in the room stopped talking when they walked in.

"Just in case," Matthews thumbed through some papers in his valise and placed them on the table, "I have these."

She didn't know what the papers were nor did she care. She just wanted this case to be over with. The bailiff told them to rise. She looked back at Birdie as the judge walked in.

The judge banged the gavel to start the proceedings. He propped his elbows on the desk as he looked around the room.

"I have been on this bench for twenty years, and this is the first time I have come across a case like this. On one hand I have a woman charged with the attempted murder of two men. If it were like all the other cases I have dealt with I could give a sentence today and be done with it, but there are other things to be considered here. Bailiff, are all of the people I requested to be here in this court today?"

The bailiff looked around the room. "Yes sir. I do believe they are all here."

"On the other hand I have a woman who thought she was protecting a friend in danger. Either way, she did shoot a man in an alley. She does admit that, and there are two witnesses to the shooting. One is the brother of the victim, and the other is the woman that was accosted that got this whole thing started. After hearing all that was said yesterday I had my marshals do some checking on the testimony of the defense witness." He pecked up a piece of paper and looked at it. "Is Big Jake in the courtroom today?"

"Yes sir, I am."

"I believe that you told me that the Indian woman Miss Perez was your property, did you not?"

"Uh...yes sir I did. I paid good money for her a while back."

"Would you please come up here?"

"Yes sir." Big Jake walked up to the bench.

"I am placing you under arrest."

"What for?" Big Jake bellowed. "I ain't done nothing." "You have been buying Indian women and using them as slaves to prostitute for you're gain. I am placing you in the custody of the U.S. Marshal."

"You can't do that." He looked at Major Wilson. "Major Wilson, do something or I'll tell them everything."

The major knew that if Big Jake talked everyone involved would be arrested. If he and the sergeant left they might have a chance to get back to the fort where they could stall the process and get a transfer back to the east and be in the clear.

"Marshal, get this man out of my sight." The judge watched the deputy marshal walk Big Jake out of the courtroom. "Stop right there, Major Wilson. I want to talk to you."

The major and the sergeant kept walking toward the door until the deputy marshals at the door drew their pistols.

"Deputy, I am major in the United States Cavalry. I demand that you step aside and let us through."

"I am ordering you back to the bench, major," the judge said.

"I am an officer in the United States Cavalry, judge, and I do not have to comply with the orders."

"I am a presiding judge in the federal court of this region of the United States, major, and I will not have you or anyone question my authority."

"I question the right of your authority to stop me from going back to the fort," the major shouted at the judge.

"Question my authority again and I'll have you shot for resisting arrest," the judge yelled back. "Bring them here to me."

The marshals escorted the two men to the front of the room.

"Major Wilson, I find it most reprehensible when men in your position not only don't uphold the law they have sworn to follow but make their own law for their own gain. I am charging you with selling Indian women into slavery. This nation is just now healing after many years of bitter fighting about the slavery issue. I am personally astounded that as an officer during the war you fought to stop slavery then you use that vile and inhumane offense for monetary gain. It has come to my attention that you have also undertaken a most complex scheme to deprive the defendant Miss O'Callahan of her property."

"What?" Rachel asked Mathews.

"Hush." Mathews waved his hand at her.

"It seems that you have placed a lien on her property

under the guise of an investment company from Salt Lake City. You also issued an illegal quarantine against her cattle to keep her from selling them. I also have a written confession from a corporal that you ordered him and another soldier to start a range fire to burn the defendant out."

"You god damned son of a bitch," Rachel jumped up from the chair and yelled at him.

"Mr. Mathews, please keep your client quiet."

"Yes sir." Mathews put his arm on Rachel's shoulder. "Rachel, sit down."

"That son of a bitch tried to steal my ranch," Rachel said.

"I know, but please sit down."

The judge waited for Mathews to calm Rachel down. "I have notified the Provost Marshal in Carson City that you will be escorted to the stockade there to wait for court marshal. Deputy, please take the major and the sergeant from the court." He waited until they were gone. "Now I must give my decision about the case at hand. Miss O'Callahan, please stand up."

Rachel and Mathews stood up.

"You have admitted in your own words to shooting Mr. Hadley Corchoran. I find you guilty. Even though you shot Mr. Corchoran, I understand the premise of why you did it. I am placing you on probation for a period of not less than five years," he waved his finger at her, "providing that you stay on that ranch and keep that shotgun unloaded." He banged the gavel on the desk. "This trial is over."

Chapter Forty

"All aboard." The train conductor took his watch out of his pocket and looked at it when the engineer blew the whistle. He waved the green and red lantern up and down to make everyone on the platform get on the train.

Rachel followed Birdie, Rosa, and Little Rachel up the steps to the rail car. She shoved the valise under the seat. "I'll be home tonight."

"Are you sure you don't want me to stay with you?" Birdie knew Rachel was going to give the deed to the ranch to Mathews.

"No. I have to do this myself." Rachel turned to leave.

Birdie grabbed her arm. "I know this is very hard for you, Rachel." She kissed Rachel on the cheek. "I want you to know that no matter whatever happens I'll be with you."

Rachel kissed Birdie on the lips. "That's all I need to know."

Rachel watched the train until it disappeared before walking up the hill to Mathew's office. She wondered what kind of incense he had in the bowl as she walked up the steps. She took the deed from her shirt pocket and read it, touching the names of her father and mother on the paper. What would they think of her? All the work they had done to make a working ranch to give it to Jacob and her. Jacob's untimely death meant that she would be responsible to continue the legacy and now she couldn't keep it. She wiped tears from her eyes. "I'm sorry, Pa and Mama. I didn't mean to let you down. I'm so sorry...."

"Who's out there?" Mathews opened the door. He could see the tears in her eyes and walked back into the room.

She wiped her eyes with her shirt sleeve before following him. "We've have some unfinished business."

"The trial is over and there's nothing left to do." He waited until she had closed the door. "You should be on your way home."

"Here is the deed to your ranch." She put the paper on the desk.

"I don't want your ranch, Rachel." He poured a glass of brandy and offered it to her. "I don't know anything about cows or alfalfa."

She refused the brandy. "I can't pay you any other way."

"Oh, but you already have. You see this case has been in the papers in San Francisco. You are quite the talk there right now. I was contacted by Smythe Loggins Weathersby and Olsen, a very prestigious law firm, because of the trial and they want me to help them with laws regarding ranching and mining. If it weren't for you I'd be an old man before I ever received an offer like that."

"I can't in good faith not pay you for you're services. What will you take?"

"Well for one thing," he drank the brandy and poured another one, "follow the judge's ruling and keep that shotgun unloaded. My payment, Rachel, is that I am going back home to San Francisco to practice law. Every day after trial I'll be sitting in the San Francisco's Men's Club smoking fine cigars and sipping twenty-year-old brandy instead of out here in this dust bowl. There will be a crowd of young whippersnappers sitting around me asking me about trials and laws. When they ask about how I got invited to practice at the law firm of Smythe Loggins Weathersby and Olsen I'm going to tell them about a case that involved a shotgun, testicles, and two women." He put the deed back into her hand and opened the door. "Now go home and have a good life Rachel. Have a good life."

Rachel walked through the house looking for Birdie. Rosa and little Rachel sat at the table in the kitchen.

"Where's Birdie?"

"She say she goes to springs," Rosa said. "She say you should go there."

"Don't wait on us for dinner," Rachel said as she walked out the door.

Rachel stopped Jester at the end of the big pond. She looked at the water and the meadow looking for Birdie and wondered if she misunderstood what Rosa had said.

"I was wondering if you'd come," Birdie said.

Rachel turned the horse around. "Why wouldn't I?"

"Things are different now."

Rachel wasn't sure what to say.

"It seems so long ago, doesn't it?"

"Yeah."

"Come sit with me in the meadow." Birdie walked along the edge of the pond.

"Okay." Rachel watched Birdie walk around the pond thinking about the many times they swam across the pond to make love. They would fall asleep in each others arms then wake up and do it all over again. Birdie was right. It seemed so long ago. She shook her head as if to remind herself that it really did happen.

"Are you going to join me or not?" Birdie said.

Rachel sat next to Birdie on the blanket.

"I thought it would be easier than this," Birdie said.

"I told you that as long as you are near me...."

"That may be good enough for you, Rachel, but it's not for me."

"I didn't mean anything by that, Birdie."

"You don't know how many nights I have stood outside the door to your bedroom trying to convince myself to go in."

"You should have told me."

"Rachel, don't you understand that it isn't something one

can just talk about. I know you love me. You've proven that again and again. I don't doubt your love for me. I don't even doubt my love for you."

"You're right, Birdie. I'm not sure that I understand what you are saying."

"Damn it, Rachel. I want so much to feel your arms around me and have you make love to me."

"Isn't that why we are out here?"

Birdie started to cry. "I can't."

Rachel wrapped her arms around her. "That's all right, Birdie. That's all right. You can let it all out now. No one can hurt you now." Rachel held Birdie and rocked back and forth while she cried. "Remember when we first came here? We were so young. We tried to swim around the pond, and I tired out and you had to pull me to the bank. I always depended on you to save me. I grew up so big and tall and you didn't. Everyone thought because I was so big that I was the strongest, but they didn't know how much stronger you really were. You've always protected me, Birdie. Even when we were apart you were always in my thoughts and prayers and that kept me from destroying myself. I don't care what you did or where you've been, you saved me by coming back. I wish I could make you understand that."

"It doesn't matter if I can't let you touch me."

"I'm not them. I'm me."

"I can't let you touch something as ugly as me."

Rachel kissed Birdie. "You haven't asked me."

"Asked you what?"

"You haven't asked me if I want to make love to you."

Birdie pushed Rachel's arms away from her. She undressed as she talked. "You think you could make love to this?"

"Sit down and I'll answer the question."

"What does that have to do with anything?"

"Sit down and I'll tell you."

Birdie sat down on the blanket. Rachel grabbed Birdie's hands and pulled her on top of her as she lay back on the

blanket.
"I'll make love to you for the rest of my life."

Chapter Forty-one

The cars turned to the right and crossed over the old wooden bridge. The preacher started the services when he was satisfied that everyone had arrived. Rachel O'Callahan Walker told everyone she would meet them at the ranch house later. She sat down between Rachel's and Birdie's graves.

"I'll take care of the ranch, Mama. You rest now and tell Birdie I love her."

"Would you mind if I joined you?"

She looked up when the shadow of the old man blocked the sun.

"I'm sorry to bother you. I tried to get here sooner, but with the war on and everything it is hard to get around.

"No, I don't mind. Please sit down."

"I'm sorry to hear about your mother, Rachel."

"How do you know my name?"

"I know you from a long time ago. I defended your mother at a trial. We've kept in touch over the years."

"Oh yeah...she and Birdie talked about you once in a while."

"All good, I hope." He laughed as touched the dirt on the grave. "You know they gave me a good life. I could never thank them enough for that."

"You helped them quite a bit too."

"Not as much as they did me." He pulled an envelope from the inside pocket of his jacket. "I uh...guess that I won't be here again so I must give this to you. Rachel made me promise not to give it to you until...you know. She wanted it to be a surprise."

Rachel opened the envelope. "What is it?"

"A deed."

"A deed...Mama already had the arrangements for the ranch and her possessions done by Mr. Collins in town."

"This isn't about the ranch or her possessions. This is about a mine up near the Canadian border. A mine near a town called Crawford's Landing. It seems that the mine was taken away from its rightful owner a long time ago." He smiled at her. "You are owner of a very healthy and productive gold mine. You are now a very, very rich woman."

Rachel read the deed several times. "I don't know what to say."

"Just do what your parents let me do. Live a good life, Rachel, live a good life."